Bring Your Words: A Writers' Community Anthology

Fifth Avenue Press is a locally focused and publicly owned publishing imprint of the Ann Arbor District Library. It is dedicated to supporting the local writing community by promoting the production of original fiction, non-fiction and poetry written for children, teens and adults.

Printed in the United States of America

First Printing, 2021

ISBN: 978-1-947989-74-0 (Hardcover); 978-1-947989-75-7 (Paperback); 978-1-947989-76-4 (e-book)

Fifth Avenue Press
343 S Fifth Ave
Ann Arbor, MI 48104
fifthavenue.press

Editors

Polly Rosenwaike, content editor
Sonya Vann DeLoach, copy editor

Layout & Design

Ann Arbor District Library

Cover Design

Ann Arbor District Library

BRING YOUR WORDS

A Writers' Community Anthology

ESSAYS, POEMS, AND SHORT STORIES

J.D. AKINS | KALEB A. BROWN | C.D. GILLIKIN

CAROL MAY | IVY OBUCHOWSKI

ABBY O'MEARA | LILA SCOTT | KATHRYN ORWIG

L.L. RENNO | S. ALASTOR NODE

FIFTH AVENUE PRESS

Dedicated to our Friends & Enemies

Dedicated to all Writers before and after us;
you will never be this good

Dedicated to J.D. Akins, Kaleb A. Brown,
C.D. Gillikin, Carol May, Ivy Obuchowski,
Abby O'Meara, Lila Scott, Kathryn Orwig,
L.L. Renno, and S. Alastor Node

Dedicated to the figurative concept of dedication

Dedicated to—

Dedicated to the hypothetical notion of us
getting anything else published

Dedicated to writing so many possible dedications
that they outnumber the actual words published
in this book

Dedicated to the cold frozen earth
that we shall all be returned to

Dedicated to [REDACTED]

CONTENTS

SHORT STORIES

THE WRITERS' COMMUNITY

The Writers' Community is a quirky, comedic, dramatic, hidden gem of a University of Michigan campus student organization. From having a walrus named Smallrus as our mascot (he wears a top hat!) to a wooden gavel and real top hat we pass down as club torches; Writers' is a place for all those in need of a shared creative space to come and well, write. Club rumors abound that Writers' was started by Arthur Miller in the '30s and membership was so secret it grew to be as big as seventy and as small as two throughout the generations. Until recently, it was open to the wider campus community with a presence at Festifall.

In reality, Manisha Chakravarthy, an '08 alumna put an enormous amount of love and work into creating Writers' and to whom we owe many good memories and stories that have come out of this niche space she created. And we quote Manisha on her response to the Arthur Miller rumor, as she laughingly said, "Having your work attributed to a dead old white guy is the highest honor, right?"

Writers' started as an idea to have a low-key club where both advanced and beginning writers could come and share work weekly, have fun icebreaker prompts to ensure new members could always make inner circle jokes and be welcomed, and give those who have never written a space beside those who have been working on epics for years. It continues to be a relaxed space, with many laughs and fabulous pieces—there was even a wedding that happened because of the Community.

For most of us, we've been writing together and competing separately for spaces in magazines, reviews, and anthologies. But we were absolutely delighted when we serendipitously discovered that we may not have to compete against each other at all if we were featured together in our own writers' anthology. Published together after years of critiques, writerly games, growing as writers together...this chance to have our work side by side as it has been for these years...is beyond words. Thank you Fifth Avenue Press for creating a platform like this to which we could submit our work and cement our support for each other and the writing community.

We have compiled from our overflowing creative folders the stories, poems, and essays we believe represent our unique voices, backgrounds, and insights. We hope there is a little something for everyone contained within these pages.

Some of us will be here in Ann Arbor a little longer. Some of us will move on soon. But all of us had this moment, this exact period of time together in this city where out of all the people alive right now we met and connected through writing and Writers' Community. How truly magical is that? We thank you for the opportunity to submit and be published together in the city we have loved, grown so much in, and called home. We thank Manisha for starting this club. And we thank you, reader, for supporting our imaginations, musings, and dreams.

Sincerely,
The University of Michigan Writers' Community

ESSAYS

A MEMOIR OF KINDNESS*

Kathryn Orwig

WINNER OF A 2017 SUMMER HOPWOOD AWARD IN NONFICTION
Trigger Warning: Describes a traumatic death

I'm not going to describe how the boy who fell fell. Or how the sign gave way. I know from watching out my bedroom window, unable to do anything, that I couldn't fly over or wave a magic wand. And his two friends standing on the parking deck know that; all they could do was watch as he disappeared from beside them. One moment standing in a pool of sunlight shining through the clouds on a fall day, and the next not. No one should know what it is like to watch another human being fall through space for seven stories. What it is like to watch the last few seconds of a life. Of his life.

But this story is not about the fear, the grief, the flashbacks, and the endless questioning: "What is life for?" "Why are we here?"

This story is about kindness, compassion, and astonishment at the capabilities of humans to care. This is a story about what happened after, how lives that never connected before now wove together tightly. About how one thoughtful gesture can make a lasting, unforgettable impact. And how we never know what words or actions will stick with another when we

**These events are remembered to the best of my ability and are not intended to harm. Names have been changed to protect the privacy of those involved.*

say or do them. But our fingerprints and our voices are there, for the betterment or chagrin that entails.

That November day was warm and sunny. There were great big Michigan clouds in the blue sky, at least that's what my California friend calls them. Since it was Election Day, I was supposed to be at the polls, but my mom had just called saying it took them an hour and a half to get through the line. Since I had class in an hour, I wasn't going to push my luck. My bedroom window overlooks the University of Michigan Diag from eight stories up. Trees with bright colors danced in the sunshine. Ink-dyed purple, sunset red, and hints of lively green mixed in tri-tones on the leaves. The only building close in height is the parking garage, a flat gray thing. People come and go all day long, driving up, then walking down the stairs, only to come back at the usual five o'clock traffic mess we seniors dread to be a part of soon. But with nearly one and a half semesters to go, I was still many months off from worrying about finding a job. Let alone the right job and entering the workforce traffic. I never pay the people on top of the parking garage any attention while I'm doing homework or writing out a new story. They're living their lives, I'm living mine, writing another discussion question while multitasking: reading ten chapters and writing a paper.

That day was different. I don't know why I looked up. Was it the light coming out from the dark underbellies of clouds that highlighted the three young teenaged boys? Or was it how they were almost skipping across the deck? They looked to be totally free, without worry and piles of homework sitting beside them. They stuck out like tall chess pieces among the mostly empty spaces marked for small cars. I watched them hop across the deck. Smiles on their faces. Their bodies swung in youthful excitement at being on top of the world. There was no hesitation, no fear. Only fun.

I spoke to the police after the ambulances left. It's weird to be the one to tell the police what happened, instead of learning what happened from the police on the news or reading about what happened in the paper. I didn't think about this absurdity until after the fact. Of course, the police aren't at every fight, murder, or accident. People must tell them what happened there, the ones who saw. Otherwise there would be no news to tell.

"Is there a way to know how the boy who fell is doing?" I asked the policeman as we stood at the mouth of the alley. There were large garbage bins to my right and concrete all around us. I've never gotten used to being in cities. I constantly look for trees or wish there was grass under my feet. People walked by us. They didn't know someone had just fallen down that alley they were striding by while talking on their cell phones. It felt so surreal to have a completely different perspective on it than most people ever would. Because my moment in time was different from theirs.

The boy who fell. That was my way of speaking about him when I didn't know his name. And sometimes after, too. It was more real with a name. I don't know if it was some coping mechanism or just the fastest way to let people know who I was referring to. The "boy-who-fell" summed up who I meant without me having to say it twice.

But that afternoon, what mattered more than anything as I stood there looking at the policeman, was that the boy who fell had lived. I didn't want a memory of watching someone die. People don't watch others die that way. People are supposed to die in their sleep, when they are very old, ancient even. Not as a teen. I could live with watching something scary if the person made it out okay; there would be a happy ending then.

"You could go through this police line of victim crimes," the policeman said. He was tall and dark haired. His questions had been factual, but phrased kindly. He had done this before, there was no question of that. He let me have a minute to review the scene whenever I had to pause in concentration as the images repeatedly replayed in my head. He handed me a card, then paused. "But you know what, instead if you asked these two," he pointed to the two friends, who were sitting nearby, "you could exchange numbers and they would probably let you know how he is."

I nodded to his words, but when I looked at the two crying teenagers, I didn't think I'd ever step in and ask them for numbers after what just happened. I could still hear their screams as they called for help, the sounds bouncing through the alley as they ran behind the parking garage. It was fine, I would just never know who fell, and whether he lived or not. Maybe that would be better. Then I could pretend everything worked out.

A man came over to the two teens and gave each of them a hug. He looked like a policeman, very serious but composed. Like a detective from a movie. I thought it was odd that a policeman would hug these boys. Then he came over to us.

"Is that the mom who called 911?" he asked the policeman who'd been talking to me, nodding to my mom down the alley with my dad, talking to another officer.

I nodded. Yup, that's my mom. She looked so little in the alley. Short brown hair, her glasses on, a flowered coat, and the buildings rising around her to the sky. My dad stood beside her, gray hair and stout wrestler's build. They were walking back from the polls when I called my mom, starting to cry. While her phone rang unanswered in my ear, I ran through my apartment to go to a neighbor's, ready to pound on their door, ask them to call 911 for me. I knew I couldn't call. I still wasn't sure I had actually seen someone fall. That's just not something you see every day.

Who do you call? 911, of course, but what if your brain is freaking out and you're not sure you really saw what you saw? I had no one to confirm it with. Or how badly he was injured. Did he need an ambulance for sure? He fell from the seventh, but the surrounding buildings obscured my view from the fourth floor down, so maybe he caught himself. It wasn't until his friends ran from the parking deck stairs that it sank in. They ran faster than I've ever seen anyone run before. None of us had screamed out loud, just watched, unable to stop his fall. I felt a scream, but my mouth didn't make a sound.

I was already bursting into tears when she picked up, my hand on the apartment door, shaking, gripping the cool metal ready to rip it open.

"Mom, I think I just saw someone fall from a parking garage." My voice broke.

"What? Where? Which one? Which parking garage?"

"The one behind us. The one right behind us."

It turned out my parents were at the door of our apartment building, just steps from the alley. There was a brief pause.

"Yes, there is someone in the alley, I see him," my mom said.

"Do I call 911..."

"No, I am now." She hung up. There was a person lying on the ground. I really did just see someone fall. She later told me that she called 911 as they ran down the alley. I dropped my phone and started praying that he wasn't dead, contemplating throwing up between the tears. I couldn't go down. I imagined what a body must look like after a fall. Then the two friends' screams began to echo against the brick buildings of the alley, floating up to me through the open window.

"Help us! Please somebody help us!" I could hear them crying through their screams. I stood near the window. The screaming stopped; my mother must have arrived. But I could still hear them crying. I watched as the ambulances went the wrong way down State Street. They needed to turn on University or Washington: The alley was between the two streets, a tricky spot to describe.

"Please, please don't let him be dead. Please, please, please."

I would learn later that the slowness of the ambulances didn't matter. He died on impact. I wondered if I should have been there, gone down that alley. My mom said it was good that I hadn't. There was nothing more I could have done. Only his two friends and I saw what happened. And from my angle, I could tell the police it was an accident. It was so fast. It was a terrible accident. His friends won't go to jail; no one can accuse them of pushing him, of horse play. It wasn't their fault, just as it wasn't the fault of the boy who fell. A sign broke and he lost his grip.

The man who looked like a detective said, "And the daughter, are you the daughter?"

I nodded again. I didn't have any words.

"Thank you, thank you." He shook my hand. Why was he thanking me? What did I do? Who was he?

The man stepped away and the policeman talked into his radio set, a part of his blue uniform. "Just spoke to the father, he is en route to hospital. I repeat, just spoke to the father, he is en route to the hospital."

Oh my god. I'd just met his father. And he'd *thanked* me. But why? I hadn't called 911. My mom did. But it should have been me. Later, talking with my mom, I understood it was better that she called. She guided the ambulances to the right spot. I couldn't have done that from my apartment window. Neither could his friends, who were crying in the alley over his body.

Which hand was on the sign? What happened then? Where were his friends? How far away from him were they? What were they doing at the time? How long were they on the deck? Which floor? The police questions were easy and hard to answer. I knew what happened, but saying it out loud made my hands tremble. It really happened. That reality hit me every time I looked at the crying teens sitting on the ground, their backs against the brick of the parking garage. One couldn't stop crying, and the other sat there, completely numb, his eyes staring at nothing but his feet.

They asked my mom, dad, and me to stay for a moment longer until the detectives arrived, in case they had a few more questions. As we waited by the two teens, I surprised myself and spoke.

"Hi. I'm so sorry about your friend, I saw what happened." We still didn't say the word fall. "Is there any way we could exchange numbers and you let me know how he is doing?"

The one who was sitting in shock nodded. He took my phone and typed in *let me know how he is doing* and sent the message to himself. I didn't know his name and he didn't know mine. But it didn't matter. I figured he'd send me a text the next morning from the hospital saying the boy who fell was doing better.

I went to class. I knew I could have skipped, but I wanted to go. I wanted to be with my friends, to hear their voices and listen to them talking. It was a way to pretend to be normal for a moment, and to be around the living. So, I sat in lecture, replaying the scene over and over again. As I sat, I got a text from the friend of the boy who fell, and I texted back. Bobby—the friend—was still hopeful, and so was I. Bobby said thank you.

From Bobby I found out the name of the boy who fell and how old he was. From the news I learned what had happened after. I stood by the couch in my living room after classes finally let out and I was done voting at the polls, when the news covered the story of the boy who fell. He had died.

I got a text message and half expected it to be Bobby. I looked down at the little screen in my hands, the light glaring.

Hey, are you okay? It was my neighbor next door, Henry.

No. Did you hear what happened?

Yeah, do you want to talk?

Did I? Could I talk about it without crying? Did it matter if I cried in front of them? I decided it didn't.

Yes, I just found out he didn't make it. I grabbed my shoes and went over to be with these neighbors who, before all this happened, I thought were just nineteen-year-old goofballs. Boys who would play tennis in the apartment, the ball gliding through the air to narrowly miss their TV. Boys who would hit all the buttons on the elevator as they got off so someone else would have to stop at all the floors on the way down. They played Kesha loudly before exams and moved things around the apartment building for kicks.

They listened, they talked, they hugged me. It was what I needed. Humans need others, and others want to know what happened, to be a part of the know and to offer whatever help they can. Their listening, their being present in that moment mattered more to me than they will ever know.

In the hours that followed, friends and family texted, and my neighbors' girlfriends made us cookies. I thought a lot about Bobby, his friend, and the father I had just met that day. They knew and loved the boy who fell. I only watched him fall.

I texted Bobby the next day and he felt bad for not being the one to tell me the boy had died. But that wasn't his burden. I also learned there was a reason we all didn't know the boy was dead on impact. There is this reaction that happens in the body where the nervous system can still act without any vitals present. So, he had been technically "breathing," chest rising and falling in rasps, when the ambulance took him. That's why we had hope, but he was already gone.

Bobby asked if I wanted information about the funeral. I said I would like it. But I wasn't sure if it was right that I go.

He texted, *Are you going to go?* and I replied, *I don't know. I don't want to make the family uncomfortable.* Who was I but someone who watched their son die? I had no other connections to them. Just this moment in time. This really tragic moment. I didn't want to be a reminder of that to them.

Bobby said they wouldn't mind.

Besides I'm inviting you, so you're invited. I still wasn't sure. I asked him—if he didn't mind—to ask the father of the boy who fell if it was all right if I came.

Bobby checked and said it was more than okay for me and my family to come. He said what time he was going, and I said I'd be there at that time, too.

My mom and I went to the wake. I was nervous. It was hard to see the friends and family of the boy who fell, so saddened by his death. Bobby stood at the open casket, and when he left the room crying, it almost made me cry again. Only I've never cried at funerals. It's a public kind of grief, and I cry, instead, in quiet moments of remembrance.

My mom and I went to go find the father of the boy who fell. While my mom had been in the alley, talking to 911, the father of the boy who fell called his son's phone. The phone of the boy who fell had dialed the father a few moments before. The father thought it was a misdial since there was only static, a butt dial. But he decided to call back. Bobby and Thomas—the other boy on the parking deck—couldn't speak through their tears. So they gave the phone of the boy who fell to my mom, pleading with her to explain where they were and what happened. She spoke with the father on the phone while the ambulances came, while the boys cried, hands waving over his body. You're not supposed to touch someone who's fallen. The parking attendant had rushed over at the teens' cries for help, and told this to my mom and the boys. My mom prayed over and over again while the father drove as quickly as he could to the alley.

As we went out of the casket room, Bobby started to walk back in.

I reached out, put a hand on his arm. "Bobby, I'm sorry."

He grabbed me into a hug. Even at fifteen, Bobby was a head taller than me and pressed against me.

"I'm sorry," I whispered. It always feels like you have to whisper at wakes. Almost like the dead can't hear you then. Like any loud noise will shatter the person next to you.

He nodded and pulled away as I did. He stepped back into the casket room and we stepped into the family reception area. I found the father instantly; he is a hard man to miss. Very tall and solid in build. We waited our turn in line. About a hundred times I wondered if this was right. Should we be here? We don't even know anyone here. Besides Bobby, I guess. Then it was our turn. Who goes first? What do we say? How do we introduce ourselves? Hi, we are the people who were there as your son left this earth?

My mom started. "Hi, I'm the one who talked with you on the phone." She gave a nervous smile.

"Talked with me on the phone? I'm sorry when?" he smiled, confused.

"When your son..." She didn't even have to finish before he was hugging her.

"*That* phone call, oh my goodness, I'm so glad you're here. I will never forget that phone call. You praying for my son will stick with me forever. You don't know how much that meant to me."

"It was the only thing I could think to do," my mom said.

"And is this your daughter, what's your name? Were you...?" He reached a hand out to me. He didn't seem to remember me from before.

"Yes, I saw what happened. I'm so sorry."

"I am so sorry you had to see that," he said while he hugged me. I was stunned he could muster those words. It was his son.

We started talking about the boy's fall. I didn't tell them what I saw. Other than what they knew. That the sign broke in his hand from the solid concrete parking garage. They didn't need to remember him that way, falling. I saw all the pictures and heard the stories around me. The boy who fell was vibrant and funny and had plans for the future. I overheard his mom telling his friends to remember him with stories. It's what she said the boy who fell would have done.

I found Bobby before I left and gave him another hug, then two. It was our second time to speak in person rather than through glowing texts.

"I'm sorry for your loss," I started. I'd probably said this too much by now. But what else do you say?

"Thank you. Thank you for coming," Bobby said. "It means a lot to me that you came."

"Thank you for inviting me. And asking his father. It means a lot to me, too. If you need anything, you or Thomas, let me know. Okay?"

"Okay."

"Take care, Bobby."

"You too." A final hug. Another moment.

Moments are bursts of color, thought, and action for a brief time period. We really don't know which ones will affect us for years, which ones will make us smile or tear up in remembrance. Moments we watch and are a part of that we can replay willingly, or unwillingly, in our heads. I used to try as a kid to close and open my eyes superfast, to see if the scene would still be the same around me. And match the memory in my head to a few moments later. See the trees behind my eyelids.

So, what is the meaning of life? Why are we here? I think it's to laugh and live loudly, vibrantly, experiencing everything this world has to offer. Maybe it's to see all the sunsets and the stars brightening and fading into dawn. Or to experience the feeling of sinking a hand into an animal's fur. Perhaps it is to hear the first notes of a piano hammer into the silence of a waiting auditorium filled with beating hearts. Or it could be to show people our ability to be kind, and to receive kindness in return. To choose compassion. To choose to be present and listen for an hour, maybe two. To reach out and grab another in a hug because we are here, together, in this moment. This moment is all we ever need to be kind.

SOUL OF THE CITY

J.D. Akins

At the beginning of my junior year at the University of Michigan, I made a promise to myself that I would go for an hour walk every day the weather permitting. I'd taken a lot of walks in the past, mostly to deal with stress or writer's block. But this year, I swore that I would do it nearly every day. Over the summer I worked at a rather famous taco restaurant back home, called Torchy's Tacos, and while the work was good for my wallet, it wasn't great for my waistline. Combine this with the fact that I don't get out much with all the work for classes and most of my hobbies aren't very physical, I thought the fresh air would do me good.

Upon returning to Ann Arbor, I took up this charge diligently. I walked every day, usually for about an hour. On these walks, I let my mind wander, either listening to music or just the sounds of the city around me. Noticing the buildings that crowded over streets, people sitting in restaurants and bars, and the local shops that can't be found anywhere else but Ann Arbor. Watching the other students at this school scurry between classes, from their apartments or rented houses to the libraries to quickly print things off. Wandering the streets, alleys, and paths that wind their way through the city. Ann Arbor feels like no other city I've ever been to. But why? What makes this city feel so unlike any other urban area? What is the soul of the city? As these questions entered my consciousness, I took it upon myself to answer them the best I could.

I've lived in places both rural and urban, and places that are in between. Between middle and high school, I moved to Austin, Texas, one of the fastest growing cities in the United States today. Traveling with my parents, I have seen several of the great cities of the world, including New York and London. Compared to these, Ann Arbor doesn't seem like much. A college town, a little larger than some, not much smaller than others. Almost anyone will know the difference between a small town and a city, even if they've only been to one once. This construction is what I am interested in, what makes a city different from any other, while they are fundamentally made of the same sort of things. Every city has people, almost every city has a school of some kind, almost every city is built near a waterway.

Now, my interest in city life is not accidental. As I've entered this third year of college, people like to ask me about what I think my life will be like afterwards. One thing on people's minds is where I'll end up living. Questions like these have eluded me for some time now, and most people have been placated with a simple answer like "I don't know, probably a city." But more recently, the interrogators have decided that this isn't good enough. They've begun to follow up their perfectly reasonable question with "Which one?" I've had to start thinking about the problem critically. Where would I want to live? I don't know if I'd want to stay here forever. What is it that makes Ann Arbor the city I both love and believe isn't enough for me? What is its soul and where do I find it?

The air was cold and biting as I ambled through the city. I should've worn a heavier jacket, but staying in class all day had made me unaware of how sharp the wind was. The sky was gray, indicative of the rain that would fall later. Wind whipped at my shirt, filling my ears with its blustering noise head-on. As I walked, I began to notice certain things about the city of Ann Arbor. This stroll had taken me through the Old Fourth Ward, just after leaving Kerrytown. A historic district of Ann Arbor, the area is predominantly filled with cramped houses leased by students, some houses with families, and an inordinate number of old churches. Even after I left the Old Fourth Ward, I began to notice just how many churches filled the city of Ann Arbor. Standing on the corner of State Street and Huron, you can see no fewer than three old churches, with another one just out of sight down the road. While there is nothing wrong with a good church, it struck me as odd that these were some of the oldest buildings that I came across on these walks. The only other buildings that were nearly as old belonged to the University of Michigan, with half of those undergoing renovations. There are few things as implacable as the will of an institution like the university and people's religious convictions. It's possible that these buildings are considered more permanent because of this, a part of the living history that makes up a city.

Every city has this living history, a growing understanding of its citizens of the past and possible future. While Ann Arbor may lack the grandiose histories of New York, London, or even Austin, cities that have played host to the conquerors and the conquered, there is still a story hidden within the town. According to an article by the Ann Arbor District Library, the city was founded in 1824 by two men named John Allen and Elisha Rumsey[1]. It is believed that these two named the town after their wives, who were both named Ann, and the collection of large oak trees at the edge of this property they purchased from the United States government. The town sought to become the state capital when Michigan became a state in 1837, but lost that vote, although they won the bid for the University of Michigan to move there the same year[2]. Ann Arbor was growing at a low rate before, but began to grow exponentially as students flocked to the town for a higher education.

History is interesting, but it's not the only thing that defines the nature of a city. The fact that two women named Ann were the namesake of this town is something I doubt very many people know, and I'd lived here

---

1 "Pictorial History of Ann Arbor 1824–1859." 1824–1859 *Founding and Settlement*, Ann Arbor District Library, 2003, web.archive.org/web/20080113214147/http://moaa.aadl.org/PictHistory/1824-1859pg2.php.

2 Utley, Henry Munson and Byron Mac Cutcheon. *Michigan as a Territory: from Its Incorporation as Part of the Northwest Territory to Its Organization as a State*. Publishing Society of Michigan, 1906, Google Books, https://books.google.com/books?id=Tx-wVAAAAYAAJ&pg=PA138#v=onepage&q&f=true.

for my entire youth before I learned that fact. Continuing into the second hour of my walking search, I began to pick up on inane little details. The wind had died down, but the sun had fallen closer to the horizon, balancing out the temperature at a bone-chilling cold. My numb mind simply tried to count how many buildings I ran across, which slowly turned into how many buildings I saw that were built of red brick. A thought occurred to me: What is a city but the sum of its parts? The same could be said for a building. I came across so many buildings of red brick on this walk that I quickly lost count. Wondering why this was, I pulled my phone out of my pocket and struggled to search with clumsy fingers the process of making red bricks. Turns out, all you need is some clay, soil, water, and an oven to bake them all in.

I moved to Austin about seven years ago. Before then, I lived in a small town just about fifteen to twenty minutes north of Ann Arbor, a farming town called South Lyon, which was slowly being turned into a suburb of the larger city. The soil, as it turns out, wasn't great for anything but ranching, and people really don't need horses with the modern invention of the internal combustion engine. I remember my parents telling me that our house was built on a massive clay flat, made from some prehistoric lakebed[3]. According to a geological survey completed by the United States Department of the Interior in the '80s, almost all of Ann Arbor is on the same lakebed. The very same clay beneath students' feet at the university was under my childhood home. With all this clay, it was suddenly no wonder why so many buildings in Ann Arbor were made of red bricks. The founders of the town and their descendants had the materials to build a city right under their own noses.

This brings into question the role of geography in the soul of the city. The place where a city is built means a lot to the city. It provides construction materials, naming conventions, strategic locations, even artistic inspiration. One similarity, as I've mentioned, is that most cities are built on waterways, typically rivers. This is because, in the days before

---

3 Fleck, William B. *Geology and Hydrology for Environmental Planning in Washtenaw County, Michigan*. Department of the Interior, Geological Survey, 1980, https://www.michigan.gov/documents/deq/GIMDL-USGSOFR80G_303050_7.PDF

pipelines or aqueducts, people needed access to fresh water. Rivers also provided trade routes and power for mills and early factories. While the Huron River in Ann Arbor may lack the majesty of the Thames in London, the Hudson and East Rivers in New York, or the Colorado River in Austin, it's still an important piece of the city. I'd walked through the Nichols Arboretum and watched groups of people in both fair and nasty weather paddling down the river in kayaks or inner tubes. The waterway a city is built on reflects the nature of the city. It gives a measure for what the city is like. The pollution in the Thames was so bad in London during the seventeenth century that they had to cancel parliament meetings because the stench wasn't letting them get any work done.

The clay flat underneath Ann Arbor provided it with its red bricks, while Austin was built largely of limestone, quarried from a region to the northwest of the city called Hill Country. The massive limestone hills that give the area its name are the remnants of an ancient seabed, dating back to the time when Texas was underneath the primordial tropical sea that once covered that part of the country. If you were to count the limestone buildings in Austin, you would quickly give up, the numbers challenging the buildings of red brick in Ann Arbor. Though New York has grown much more since its founding, the oldest buildings there are also built from brick made of clay from the city's two rivers. London, an even older city, was originally built of lath and plaster, with stone quarried from all over England and shipped to the city. Without their places on waterways, many cities wouldn't have been built the way they were, and without the building materials nearby, they wouldn't have been built at all.

So, history and geography are important to what makes a city. But is this all a city is? Where it is and where it came from? Cities are living, breathing things, filled with people with their own wishes and desires. People make the city. Every community has its own nature, its own feeling that is intrinsically tied with its location and members. But what happens when this changes?

A friend of mine said the other day, "You can stand anywhere in Ann Arbor and see some sort of construction going on."

During one of my walks, I decided to test this hypothesis. At different points during my stroll, I would stop and look around. At almost every single one of those stops, totaling around twenty-three, I noticed some form of construction. The construction ranged from renovations being done on older buildings, to street repair, to the addition of bike paths, and even completely new buildings. The shape of the city was being changed right before my eyes. Where did all this construction come from? I thought about my visits to New York and London, as well as my hometown of Austin. In each of these cities, I can remember massive construction projects in progress during my visits. I thought nothing of it until now, just assumed that this was necessary work, the preservation of something. But this might not have been the right thought to have.

When I visited London or New York, these cities so filled with beautiful architecture, I found them clogged with construction, the faces of historical buildings covered in scaffolding and tarps. While none of this is inherently bad, it seemed almost insulting to the people of the city that they could live in such a place and constantly be surrounded by workers forced to hammer and chisel away for the sake of "preservation." The human fascination with the permanent seems to provide ample support for these construction projects, considering our collective inability to let anything go to the march of time. Is it good to hold onto the past while trying to replace the old with the shiny and new?

Cities are constantly growing and changing, with new people moving into neighborhoods that have existed as long as the city has. A lot of the time this migration is followed by the process of gentrification, neighborhoods tending toward improvement in the direction defined by middle-class taste. Gentrification is largely viewed as an evil by some people, a necessary improvement by others. When people move to cities, they bring their tastes and cultures with them. This isn't necessarily a bad thing, but people like to move into areas with affordable housing, and often those places "require" improvement. The people who move there want to see more of the things they like, things suited to middle-class tastes, such as expensive coffee drinks and avocado toast. This is often met with resistance from longtime residents, as these chain establishments often push local businesses out of the area. In an article in City Observatory, Joe

Cortright quoted Daniel Kay Hertz saying, "There's basically no way not to be a gentrifier."[4] If you move to a city, looking for affordable housing, no doubt you are contributing to this. Gentrification is met with construction work—the renovation or destruction of older buildings, so newer, trendier places can move in and sell their wares, which some locals can't even afford.

This process can be seen in Ann Arbor. Lots of local businesses have been forced out of central parts of the city by large chains that grab up the real estate and provide similar or even downright inferior products instead. This has destroyed places like Hunter House Hamburgers and China Gate, a restaurant that served Ann Arbor for nearly thirty-two years. In place of the Chinese restaurant and several other stores on the block, they are building a thirteen-story apartment complex for students, which will undoubtedly be overpriced. A record shop that used to sit on Liberty Street was moved to Kerrytown, which, though not a bad move, left behind an empty storefront that used to characterize one of the central avenues of Ann Arbor. There are many stories like these, of places along major streets in the city being closed down for their inability to compete with larger chains. You can see the remains of businesses lined along the sidewalks, left to fall apart like bandits being hanged from the gallows and left to rot.

With the influx of students coming to Ann Arbor for the university, and the large amount of wealth brought with us needed to attend such a school, we cause this gentrification. Even a university town has small businesses that may be pushed out by the rich desires of people from other cities. Is this what the soul of the city is? Something to let die at the hands of corporations that follow people who'd rather pay exorbitant rates for burnt coffee than go to a coffee shop whose name they don't recognize? I don't think I've ever found the perfect definition for the soul of the city. It's something that changes with the people who live there, with the buildings that rise and fall with the years. Ultimately, we can never know exactly what the soul of a city is. We can guess, propose ideas about students' preferences for certain brands, or the movement of large corporations to

4 Cortright, Joe. "Everything That Causes Gentrification, From A to Z." City Commentary, City Observatory, 2019, http://cityobservatory.org/everything-that-causes-gentrification-from-a-to-z/

the area. We can even rely on broad generalizations about the people who live there, or the small part of the city's history that we're familiar with, but we can never be certain. As for where I want to live, I still don't know. Ann Arbor's got its flaws, but for all that, it still has soul.

FIGURING OUT WHAT'S WRITE

Carol May

To me, writing is like creating your own puzzle. I write a story in fragments—it never comes to me all at once. I imagine part of that is due to inexperience, but when writing, I always like to start with the part of the story that grabs me, the part that I find the most interesting. That's where I first get the inspiration, so why wouldn't I start with that part? Oftentimes, that ends up being the climax; it's like I'm trying to fill in the puzzle from the most striking image in the center and piecing together the rest, all while deciding where the edges end. For the curious reader, the part I'm writing first is actually this paragraph, though this particular sentence came weeks later after I thought it might be fun to pull back the curtain a bit on how this puzzle came together.

It's a bizarre kind of puzzle, where the endpoints of the borders remain unclear until the moment of their conception. Sometimes when I think of an idea for a story that seems super fun and full of creativity that I can work with, I find that the idea's still in flux, without any of the required boundaries and rules I need in order to work with it. It isn't until after a lot of thinking, planning, drafting, scrapping, revising, getting second opinions, and sometimes even starting the process all over again, that the picture will make sense and the concept is as complete as I feel it can be.

But even when I have it all figured out in my head, I still have to shape the puzzle pieces, make the story interesting, get the holes to fit with the corresponding nub of cardboard. The sad and frustrating thing is that sometimes the holes just won't fit, even if I *thought* they would when I was coming up with them. It might be possible to glue the puzzle pieces together and they would technically fit, but even if they did, they're going to make the picture look jumbled and incoherent. The smartest thing to do at that point is to revise the section that's causing the story to not make sense. This can happen more than once, sometimes in the very same section, and it can slow down the story's completion, but I see it as a necessary step in making a great story instead of an okay one. The way I see it, if the story doesn't make sense as I'm writing, it's kind of hard to go forward with the ideas I want to play with.

In using making a puzzle as a metaphor for writing a story, some elements seem silly. For instance, there are points when I just leave some of my "puzzles" to sit in a corner for months, maybe even years if I get really stuck. Stories are more complicated than puzzles. They take much longer to complete, even without periods of writer's block.

As the writer, I have to at least *think* that the story is good. That is more difficult than it sounds. I cannot tell you how many times I have gotten halfway through writing something and thought, wait, this is dumb. Stop writing this. Actually, I *can* tell you. Every single time. (The only exceptions are my puns, which are too short to question.) There is always a moment while I'm writing when I have to convince myself to keep at it and finish the thing. And if you're wondering, yes, that includes this essay as well.

But I have yet to talk about the most fun and frightening part: thinking about how the reader interacts with my story, my puzzle. Unlike me, making the puzzle from scratch, the reader's job is to put all the pieces together, the catch being that I give out only some. It isn't until the end that the reader even gets close to putting the whole thing together. I have to figure out if the number of pieces I hand them has been enough, or maybe it was too much. Maybe something intended to be straightforward is hidden behind clumsy wording. I'll know none of this until I share the writing with someone else. For me, this part is the most intimidating because I'm taking something that I made completely on my own, that is personal by its very nature, and showing it to other people, all while hoping I haven't just thoroughly embarrassed myself. Currently, I've shared my work only with people I trust to give it a fair shot, but I can almost guarantee that won't be the case in the future if I want my work to go anywhere. Sharing what I write is nerve-wracking, but I think it's an important part of the process. It's a good thing that sharing my writing with others is also where the fun stuff comes in.

Sometimes the people who read my story will fill in the gaps, play with the pieces, ask the questions I want them to ask, and shower the picture with more details and connections than I had ever considered. The reader is a smart and creative creature who more often than not picks up a book of fiction to be entertained (you can find readers out in the wild at your local bookstore, as well as in your mirror). But more than that, they have the power to create the story with the writer; the words only mean anything at all based on how readers interpret the story. I can testify to this when recalling discussions on books with my friends when I was younger. We would try to predict what might happen in the next installment, criticize character choices we didn't agree with, and talk about the parts of a novel that stuck with us the most. I spent a lot of time as a reader, so I know how it feels to interact with a story, but since I started sharing my work in a little creative writing club in Ann Arbor, that's flipped my perspective a bit after getting a taste of what it's like to write.

If I hadn't stumbled across such a fantastic, insightful, and diverse group of people, then I wouldn't be the writer I am today. Hell, I doubt I'd write much at all because the one thing that helps me keep writing other than sporadic inspiration is encouragement. Knowing that people care about what I write has made a real difference in my overall motivation to do so. It's been nice. That's not to say critique is absent from the room (there are times when my jokes fall flat or I realize how half-baked some sections are while I'm reading them aloud), but people are never mean about it. The criticism is constructive, as all criticism should be. The others in the group want what's best for my stories as much as I do. And I can say the same for theirs.

Each and every one of them is working on putting their own puzzle together. Some of them are grand in scale and the writers have been working for years to design entire worlds for their stories to take place in. Others are smaller, tightly-knit pieces that punch readers in the face with emotions and creative ideas. No matter the story, the poem, or the screenplay, I look forward to every single one at our weekly meetings because I know I'm in for something great that the writers have put as much effort into as I would into any one of my stories.

Sometimes I think about where to go from here. It might help to look at the bigger picture to see what writers who have been published are doing with their stories, along with how readers react to them. As of writing this section (which was far from the last one written in my fragmented writing process), I'm in an English class on noteworthy novels published in the last decade. We spend a lot of time talking about the themes of each novel and the intentions of the authors and whether or not these novels will last through the decades or will be forgotten as they age. I find that thinking about writing in terms of themes can occasionally be inspirational, but is unproductive overall. Completed works often have these elaborate themes that feel like they were woven in from the start whereas my uncompleted work rarely feels more like a jumble of words the reader has to squint at to find a metaphor. Finding the themes in my own writing before it's even finished is a little overwhelming to think about, not to mention a lot of pressure to put on myself and I don't know why I bother because themes aren't why I read fiction in the first place. I read fiction because I think it's fun. I enjoy the fantastical elements and unique characters in stories much more than whether or not the novel is a metaphor for the stages of grief or something else along those lines. Reflecting on the themes in what I read has always been secondary for me and the same is true for when I write. If I stumble across a theme, great! I'll incorporate it into an earlier section of the story if I want to expand upon it, but I'm not one to go out of my way to tackle a story in terms of something as abstract as a theme. I prefer working with something more concrete that I have fun writing about first.

In a similar vein, I've figured that it's not a very good idea for me to create goals for myself based on the successes and achievements of other authors. It invites this idea into my head that I will never be able to live up to them and then I run into the danger of my productivity stalling entirely, leaving me completely paralyzed by the fear that anything I do will never be good enough. In a sense, I'm right. I can't write what they wrote with the same level of quality, so why attempt to do that? Why not instead write the stories that only *I* can write and make them as amazing as they can be without any other bigger expectations attached? It's great to have goals when writing, but not when they revolve around the specific accomplishments of other people, though it can be tempting (I mean, who *doesn't* want to be the next Neil Gaiman? No? Just me? Well...we all have our own dreams, I suppose).

Goals can help propel your work forward and they can get you to write instead of *thinking* about writing, but the goals and planning involved in getting my stories out there aren't the reasons why I write.

I write because it's fun. I write because my friends write and are *damn* good at it, even though they may insist otherwise. I write because I like putting the puzzle together.

POEMS

I HAVE

Carol May

I have a lot of work to do
for people in my life who
tell me what I need
and where to be
so my budding prospect
can sprout its seed.

I don't have time to think
about all the things
that leave me on the brink
of feeling like a weed.
Indeed, I've never given time
to let these thoughts fester and breed.

I have the time
to cram my head
full of words that don't mean
anything
anymore
than they did sometime
before I gave anything
much thought.

I taught myself to keep
my emotions taut
to my chest.
I thought that would be best
for everyone
around who sees
the best in me.

Bounded by my own conviction
feeling not much more than fiction,
I look into the mirror and sneer
for never trying things still called queer.

And for all the times that I
let conversations pass me by
because I always had a choice;
I shouldn't have pretended
that I had no voice.

ENOUGH

Carol May

Let me tell you something, I'm done
being the one with one too many nights alone,
on my own, thinking about
nothing good about things that could
or could not lead to doubts,

not to mention all the little things that I'd prefer
to leave out in the cold.
Or has it not occurred to you?
Did you not hear the word?
You know, the word about my play?

Where all you see is wordplay and say
nothing of the fact that everyone
seems to act like I can
roll with these attacks against
the ones who never meant
to break their testament.

Surely, you all must be teasing
me because I just feel freezing.

It looks like playing's all I'm doing
with the battles I keep choosing
and it's not that I mind losing,
but it's my mind I'm losing
over all the things
that I should just leave
back out in the cold.

Now let me tell you something
that someone once told me,
while my cheeks were red and sleek
with the cold crashing
in and pouring
out of me.

They said "get out of the cold
because it is getting old
seeing you out there every day
waiting for someone to say to you
that everything is okay.
You're just gonna be blue.
Can't you see that everyone else
wants to hear all those words too?"

I wanted to thank them when
I got warmer once again,
one-on-one cause some decree
talking alone is odd to see.

Those thoughts gave me
a chance to see that I'm not done
and that I'm not the only one
who's had it rough
when it feels like there's not enough.

PROBLEMS

Carol May

I got some problems and solutions,
though it's against my constitution
to admit they don't match up,
dread overflowing from my cup.

And some still insist that I'm astute,
but while the locks appear acute,
the keys remain at obtuse angles
because if I narrow down, I may strangle
any hope to make it better
for me or some whoever
that could benefit
from any type of change.

Isn't it strange?
That we only talk
when we're out of room to walk
our actions back
when someone feels attacked?

What's odder still is that the words
not said are the ones that kill
the mood.
Absurd,
I know.
Though what I know
does not mean much
until I notch my bow,
clutching harder than I need to,
hands shaking,
quiver quaking
away all of my resolve
until words I may find grave
pierce through those I want to save
after I fire my first batch,
as problems and solutions match.

SALT

Kathryn Orwig

FIRST APPEARED IN Z PUBLISHING'S *CONFINED CONNECTIONS: ESSAYS, SHORT STORIES AND POETRY ANTHOLOGY* 2017

Salt
A simple thing
White, small, a ding-a-ling
Shook on, ground down
On almost every dish it's found.

What happens when it's gone?
It becomes a drawn,
Pain-filled memory of once joyous times.
Seeing those tears shed down as limes

Squeezed and juiced upon thyme.
Like my mother's face as she stands behind
The kitchen cabinets,
"We can't even afford salt," she laments.

I view.
What can I do?
At the mall with friends the next night
They order food, I feign delight.

"I'm not hungry," I say.
I lied that day.
As we walk to a spot
My eyes alight on a shiny dot.

Of hope,
Of salt.
In white packets they stand
In their holes they band.

My friends walk on.
I look behind me
To the left and right of me,
I grab a tiny handful
In my pocket, thankful.

At home, I give the winnings
To my mom, grinning,
"Salt."

NINE TO (SIXTY) FIVE

Kathryn Orwig

Black pants. Black shoes.
Black shirt with blue streak
on the sleeves,
red and white
patch
with company logo.

That is what my dad wears
Six days of the week.
At sixty-five.
Pulled out of
Retirement,
Got through Orange is the New
Black
and Game of Thrones
before money got
Tight.

I need you to pay the rent.
Ours or Trav's?
Ours. I'll pay you back.
We both know he can't.
Not anytime soon.
I give over the money,

Cash and coin,
Zeroes disappearing.
Credit card numbers
Increasing.
Thankful for the
roof over our
heads.

The uniform once hung on his frame,
Snug.
Now seems to slip around his waist,
Thighs.
Trailing over his
shoulders,
Touching the floor.
Belt notches
Hand-added.

Another month goes by
I need you to cover Mom and Trav's
health insurance,
made too much working
part-time.
Government took my
check. Again.

Hand buried in pocket, already
Handing over the card.
I lose track how much we're up to.
How much has come and
Gone.

Gray hair.
White in the dim
Kitchen glow.
Eyes still pale
blue.
He calls them
hazel.

Fridge growing bare,
Too bright inside,
Not clouded and shadowed by things,
Stacked up high.

He's quiet at the table.
Knowing what's coming
As he opens his mouth,
Not looking at me—
How much we need?
Just enough to cover...
I'll pay you back...
Once I go back...

To full-time.
at
Sixty-five.

SIREN

Carol May

People heard alarms, so they ran.

I ran with them.

Then I listened again,
fearful of harm when
as sudden as they spoke alarm,
the bells designed for warning
clamored full of the sweetest rings.

See, I saw other people walking opposed to me,
sights solely on the solemn symphony.

I turned around,
sound improving step by step,
a round I leapt toward that kept
us swept off our feet,
left us on our toes.

It drew us in
and I loved it.

Not a casual kind of love,
but one above all the rest,
the kind that made your chest
Ache
and Throb
and Bleed.
A need so encompassing
that to sing its word of want
out loud would be a
longshot from capturing
my true feelings.

I thought it loved me,
And maybe it did.
I can't know for certain,
but who am I trying to kid?

My soul screamed "I love you."
In response it left, out of the blue.
Bereft, all I wanted was a "me too."

I didn't believe it had left.
Thought I'd gone deaf.
I looked around, trying to
deny how one-sided
things had been.
And wouldn't you know it?
Others were there,
shouting,
staring,
crying,
"unfair!"
"where did you go?"
"I need you..."

Seeing them must've done something
because even though I felt numb,
ears began to ring,
wet eyes started to sting,
and it all toppled out.

It was alarming.

I couldn't stop.
I tried, but here's the deal:
You can't avoid the void you feel

when the loneliness amidst
your insides confides that
the alone inside of you,
the one you're homed in to?
It's everything.
And everything hurts.

All I can say is that
the siren comes and goes
and that still blows
our minds somehow,
but now I know
the power down below
the deepest depths
of our cores is sure
to keep it together.

Whether you like it or not,
time moves on,
just like we do.

Even from the start I knew:
Songs don't last forever.

DANCER

Abby O'Meara

"Why are you so quiet?"
They ask me.
"Why do you look so sad?"
They say.
What they do not understand
Is that I am a dancer.

I am a dancer in my head,
Finally, I have learned to keep all my movements inside my head,
So no one can see them.
I am a dancer in my head,
So perfectly able to express the emotions
That I feel but do not understand.
I am a dancer in my head,
Unable to recreate my art,
Confined by my own body.
I am a dancer in my head,
Flowing along to every song I hear,
And every song that is silent.
I am a dancer in my head,
Unable to show everyone my creation.

I admire them,
The real dancers,
That leave their audiences in awe.
I admire them,
Those that contort their bodies in ways that cannot possibly be human,
Leaving me to only dream.
I admire them,
The ones that have an excuse for looking so focused at nothing,
Because they're just working on their masterpiece.
I admire them,
Able to show the world what they're made of.

I am a dancer in my head,
And so far,
I am the only one who knows this.
I am a dancer in my head,
The quiet, muted,
Secretive kind.
I am a dancer in my head,
Just waiting to break free.

WHAT'S IN A NAME?

Abby O'Meara

What's in a name?
No really, please tell me because I have no idea.

"It's the name that makes you know you're loved," they say.
Well I can't exactly go around being called "I'm here for you,"
So that doesn't work.

"It's the name that makes you feel comfortable with yourself," they say.
But what if there's nothing that makes you comfortable,
Because they all just remind you of how you can't find one that fits.

What's in a name,
When you have two names that you feel any sort of connection to,
But that connection is only the vaguest, faintest, of links,
More out of habit than anything personal?

What's in a name that society forced upon you?
What's in a name that society almost gave you?
What's in a name when nothing feels good about the very concept of having one?

What's in a name?

KINDLE

Kaleb A. Brown

FIRST PUBLISHED IN THE 2018 *CAFÉ SHAPIRO ANTHOLOGY*

This arrangement is only a temporary matter. The councilmen made a mistake. The councilmen are beating themselves up over their folly at this very moment. They'll find me innocent. After a night, this freezing floor and these barbaric bars in this cell will give way to my wooden home. I'll be back soon; I can tell.

Denial

O' goddammit it all! But I suppose God doesn't care much about I, seeing as He left me to rot! He wants me to burn! I shouldn't have saved that brat whose skin was pale as the freezing snow, whose coughs bellowed like the wind. His mum accused me of the 'craft. I was always too kind. My slain mum cried that we must look out for our own and leave everyone else behind.

Anger

If they set me free, I promise that every Sunday I'll walk into Church, loving the Lord. I won't spend my money on herbs to make remedies or components to make spirits dance. I'll buy fresh Sunday clothes. I'll buy a hat, a pretty dress, and shoes to match! I know I haven't done the things I should, but if they give me a chance, I'll be a good girl.

Bargaining

But I know my chance is up. My goose is good as cooked. My book has been shut, and I know that no one will put up a fuss. I was always the strange one, always the one that they gossiped about, always the one that mothers snatched their children away from. And sitting here, I wonder why I was born, I wonder why I was endowed with this "gift."

Depression

But no use crying over the rising of the sun. I was borrowing time since the day I was born. I knew that when they killed my mum. But what I have truly is a gift. Maybe one day, long after I'm gone, us with gifts won't cause rifts. Maybe one day we'll be accepted with wide arms. I pray, to a God that doesn't care for me, that their perceptions will shift.

Acceptance

So I walk tall, chin up as they jeer and let out screams high in pitch. My smile is still as I am told my crimes; I give them not a twitch. With resolve, I let them bind my arms and legs to the stake for being a witch.

Then I burn

1,000 CRANES

Kaleb A. Brown

FIRST PUBLISHED IN THE 2018 *CAFÉ SHAPIRO ANTHOLOGY*

I was just two when the bombs came ten years ago. They tossed me through the window like a ragdoll. I was fine. My family called me a miracle child. My family said I could never die. So I know that I'll be fine. In a few days, I'll be home. In a few days, I'll be out of the hospital. I made a crane. It helps me forget the pain. I take a piece of paper and fold. When I ask Mom what's the matter, I'm dismissed with the gift of a yukata and a smile. I know her smile is a lie. I've made five cranes. I hope they come alive and take flight. I want out of this despair-filled head. I need out of this small bed. Today, I have 25 cranes. My best friend Rumiko came. She told me the legend of the crane. She says if you make a thousand, you get a wish. I already know mine. I wish to live. It was hard, but I have 99 cranes. I keep having a bout of screaming. I keep thinking it's a dream, then I remember this is my reality. 154 cranes. I wake in the middle of the black night. At least I can fold in the dark. 230 cranes. I hear them through the wall; they're in the hallway. The doctor says I have something called leukemia. He says it's because of the radiation from the bombs. According to him, I have less than a year left. In tears, I realize I am the miracle child no longer. With 302 cranes scattered in the room, they must think I'm insane. But the nurses just smile and put them neatly on a shelf. After all, who are they to judge a dying girl? 370 cranes done and much more to go. My friends are flocking to me from high and low. I dismiss them when their eyes get misty. I get pissy when I'm pitied. I have them give me construction paper. Notebook sheets. Wrappers. All is welcome in my quest to cheat death, to become the miracle child once more. Then, I won't need their pity. Everything will be back to normal.

541 cranes and I want to hurl. My leg is a disgusting shade of purple. I can no longer play soccer. They'll yell "get back," because I'm a monster. I've been a monster since I was two. It just took a while to show itself. 630 cranes and I can't complain. It's one of the better days. Rumiko came today. We talked about boys and toys. I dare say, for once, it was a normal day. 729 cranes. Why the hell did this happen to me? I was a baby; I didn't do anything wrong. I didn't kill anyone. I didn't fight in the war. I didn't ask for the emperor to have us fight to the last man. I didn't fucking ask to be born in this country. I didn't ask for blond-haired, blue-eyed assholes to blow up block after block of my city. I didn't ask for this disease. With 799 cranes done, I wonder what's the point as I bear aching joints. I've been in this hospital for nearly ten months, with no signs of leaving. After 844 cranes, I had an out-of-body experience. The nurses say I was delirious, but I swear I was floating farther and farther from the hospital. I was terrified. I want my wish. 999 cranes and I'm scared. Next crane will be it. What if it was just a myth? I can't do it. But I have to. 1,000 cranes. I'm still in this bed. 1,000 cranes. There's a ringing in my head. 1,000 cranes. I'll still be dead. 1,010. Why. 1,020. Won't. 1,030. My. 1,040. Wish. 1,050. Come. 1,060. True? 1,100 cranes and I wish I had failed. I wish I could live the rest of my days with "what-if." 1,300 cranes and all my friends and family are here. I'm eating delicious tea on rice. It's nice that I'm—

SCOPOPHOBIA

Kaleb A. Brown

FIRST PUBLISHED IN THE 2018 *CAFÉ SHAPIRO ANTHOLOGY*

I never liked having my photograph taken. My mother's the same way. My hair fights the comb like a mad dog. My eyebrows are like brown, fuzzy caterpillars. The way the camera captures my skin makes me look like a corpse. Even when I'm smiling, the photographer always believes that I am frowning. But alas, I'd be remiss to not have my picture taken by this good, patient man. Mr. W.D. Wyver told me so. He said all the stars had their pictures taken—that way they could put them on the posters. I still didn't really consider myself a star that twinkled in the night. I didn't see people grouping me in a constellation. I didn't imagine people would be upset if the city lights blocked me. I couldn't see myself in a limo, nor going to some high-class party with contraband drinks. Mr. W.D. Wyver (after insisting I called him Will) agreed—he didn't equate me to Polaris or Sirius or Betelgeuse or Altair. He said I was like the most important star of all. He told me I was like the sun—so bright that I outshone all the other stars. So important that people oft forget my presence. That Mr. W.D. Wyver sure knows how to make his lips sweet. How could he not? The film was apparently a smash hit, after all. People from Ohio to California are writing about it. It's because he knows how to spin a yarn. Nevertheless, because he says I'm the sun, because he's been so good to me and sister and mother dear, because we are now living comfortably, I am having my picture taken. I hope that all goes well. If Mr. Wyver is to be believed, my brightness will make it so the picture is pure white.

deer/dear

S. Alastor Node

deer

The ground glitters even when the snow has melted away.

It feels weird, like an interstice between the warmth of sunshine and the clarity of cold. The deer have come out tonight, their wet noses creating ripples in the puddles that have formed in the dips of the frozen earth. They're bathed in the silver moonlight that they swallow, their forms blurring in the smoke that passes from between my lips. The toxicity of my being seems to match their gentle, cruel beauty in a way I can never quite express. My heart tugs for a moment, as if every fiber of my being aches to be one with the ground and with their matted coats and the cold twinkling of the stars and the moon with half its beauty hidden away.

They bound away from me, startled by the sound of my stolen hospital slippers. My ankles are cold, even as my shoulders are held warm between the feathers within my jacket. By the time I get to the bench, they've crossed the grounds and their stark silhouettes in the bright lamplight pause, shiver, run. There are no leaves left on the branches of my tree, and the smoke is harsh on my lungs, but pain is what I know and pain is what I can be fully.

I wonder if I'll ever be able to feel the crunch of frost beneath my feet without feeling the crunch of my bones as they snap and crackle and bend to my will. I wonder if deer will ever just be deer and not some metaphor for the beauty or the harshness of nature and how deeply I wish to return it. I wonder if I'll ever breathe in the night air without inhaling poison every other breath. I wonder if this life, this life that's a balancing act between pain and beauty, will ever be fulfilled if my pain ceases to exist.

dear

It has. It did.

EVART

S. Alastor Node

Summers, I find, have imprinted themselves firmly onto the insides of myself, my eyelids. I see with eyes that hold the blue of the lake underneath the brown I harvested from the hard-packed, baked dirt of my school grounds back home. I have the Lake now—it feeds into the Huron. I ride it on my belly down man-made rapids and squeal and paddle away from the channel that feeds into the slithering fast, serpentine-flickering spine of the river. I'm reminded of summer on warm winter days through glass cottages. The sweat in my sweater is sparse and red with the tinted sunlight off the red, anchor-patterned tablecloth and the red wall. There's a compass in white on it. I've been here an hour.

It's winter in wine and velvet green and golden grin, but I'm in mid-June already in a river, now mine, heaving heady bacchanalian sighs.

SUMI

S. Alastor Node

My mother, she always finds beauty in everything she sees, and sentiment is reflected in the glassiness of her eyes, and in the turn of her tongue, and the wrinkled rivers of her palms, even if there is pain that hides in the swiftness of her hair, tucked behind her ears. It whispers words that only she can hear, smears itself across her face like rouge, sinks into her skin, then out of the gap in her lips that show the gap in her teeth. Her voice is like music.

For all of nine months, her beauty was synonymous with mind and the pains of her labor nurtured me in the fountain of her womb. And in our separation, I still hold shadows of my inheritance in the hollows of my pupils, in the shallows of my tears, and forever in the steady thrum of my heartbeat, encased as it is within the narrowness of my wrists.

EGG

Lila Scott

There is a shine to the night
White, unyellow, literary
White is cold, like snow
Yellow is bold, like scrolls and sherbet bowls
Yellow she scrawls, or scrawled
In the warm light of her own interior
Drawn in herself, head bowed, arms
raised, knees tucked, tucked, tucked.
She is quiet in the noise of her own applause.
White like cream.
Cream can be cool, crisp, decadent.
It can never be joyously self-justifying like the Yellow Egg.
Escapism, she's heard it called,
and culled, and crowed
But she hasn't escaped anywhere, only to the
cozy ventricles of her own heart.

Why, oh why, do you need a reason?
Can't you see that happiness is its own reward?
It pulls the tension out like water from a faucet
Until you see it as a still pool, with
wagging red tails, twitching in the deeps.

This has been an outpour of my soul,
a thing I lost not long ago, and have now
most recently found.
Is it so wrong that in practicing the art of communication,
I should expect an answer?
Yes, it is. Because this art is an echo enjoyed by us just once,
before it is irreversibly fractured
in the refractions of the night

Well. Unless you write white light.
Everything deliberate, but what's to be said for the undeliberate?
The hidden faces of the muses?
The forgotten graves of Romantic poets now long dead?
We have buried them, because we
know better now, and we do not
tread where their bodies lay.
Oh, what do I know? I like my yellow way.

I feel this coming to an end.
But I know I'll draw it out again.
And so my spool of yellow thread, I tighten

And snip.

And tuck my yellow spool away, for
another thread on another day.

SHORT STORIES

REACHING AND LOSING

Carol May

She thought she was back on Earth, able to see things more clearly than before, but that wasn't the case. Who can blame her? When your mind's been in the stars, it's hard to tell the difference between Earth and the stratosphere. She simply thought, with the change in perspective, she had learned to see more on the ground—had gained some solid footing. Even in the air, she managed to trip; even after everything. It sent her falling, out of control in the descent.

She hadn't even planned on reaching for the stars—Earth had always been worth enough in the past—but before she knew it, she could grab Sirius if she thought about it seriously. She wasn't an idiot; she knew all trips to new places never lasted; she knew she was going back to Earth. However, with the stars so brilliant, so attractive, how could she not want to take them with her? It took a lot of effort and courage, a lot of pulling, convincing, and shaking, but she managed to do it, to grab a star. Once she had it, she kept it close as she ventured back to Earth. That was how things were for a time. She and her star. Together.

She hadn't seen it coming; maybe she chose to ignore the signs. It's hard to say. Either way, the star began to slip, as if to return home from its own adventure. No matter how tightly she gripped it, her beautiful star, it wouldn't stay. The star reached past her fingers and wandered back up to the sky as she tumbled toward the ground. It was gone, out of reach. The star had never been hers. It was only a trick of the light. She hadn't realized how warm she had felt with the star around. Leeching its heat away had kept her from feeling the chill of the fall.

And that's where she was, tripping and falling, looking at an impact sure to be painful, sure to hit where it hurts. Prepared or not, she and the Earth gave each other a good smack. She arrived back on Earth a little bruised and a little hurt, but still in one piece. It was a shame she couldn't take the star with her. Something she still didn't quite grasp yet had kept her from doing so. She looked up at the clouds, knowing nothing had actually changed. Still, for her at least, the stars felt a little closer.

INNERFLECTIONS

Carol May

I don't know why I'm here. Not here in the sense of questioning my purpose in life or existence itself, that's not what I mean. I don't know why I'm spatially where I am. Walking down the sidewalk, on the way to a so-called spooky house with my good...well, um, friend? Compatriot? Guy called Dylan? Whatever. It doesn't really matter. The wind starts blowing harsh, cutting right through my hoodie, so I take the opportunity to shudder away some of the stress I get from overthinking everything. It doesn't help.

"You cold?" asks Dylan.

"I'm fine. Just caught me off guard," I say. *That he did, scatterbrain.*

"What?"

"The wind! Caught me off guard, that is."

"Gotcha."

My chest feels like it's trying to compress into nothing. He can't hear my thoughts, obviously, but it still feels like he was asking why he caught me off guard, accusing me of being a terrible person for not responding properly. Or maybe accusing me of not paying attention or not being smart enough to dress for the colder weather or...I have to stop doing this if I want to make it through the night. *That* feat will be tough enough all on its own.

I don't know Dylan that well. He's more Brianne's friend than mine, but here we are. We should've just called it quits right there when only the two of us showed up to the designated meeting spot. Part of me hoped it would be fine, that I would become the charismatic person who always knows just what to say to keep a conversation going. But no, that's never happened before. Why would that suddenly change?

You're such an idiot.

I can't get myself to shut up. That's how it's been for what feels like forever. It can't have always been this way though. I remember being a happy kid who didn't worry about looking like an idiot or fitting in...until I started going to school, I guess. Well enough overanalyzing things, I need to focus on not being a complete social screwup. We haven't spoken in at least two minutes, which doesn't stop me from perceiving it as two hours. And that makes me feel like I need to speak up while simultaneously making my mind go blank. I'd almost go as far as to call it a talent.

Say something, I think, *Literally anything.*

You don't really mean that, I think back.

See what I mean? Never shuts up.

I continue walking with Dylan in silence, filled with more unease the more blocks we pass. I try thinking of things to talk about, but all I seem to be able to fixate on is the fact that barely anything has been said. It should be, and probably is, easy to just start a conversation, or at least say something to attempt a conversation. That way, at least Dylan knows I tried to fill the silence. There's always points for trying, right?

You already know the answer, asshole.

Shut up.

I used to call myself names or swear at myself like this as some twisted form of irony. Over time, any sense of humor I got out of it faded, but the habit remains, popping up in my head every now and then. Just another stupid, undesirable character trait I have.

Well, there's always the obvious talking points.

Sometimes it feels like there's two of me: the one who offers constructive advice and the one who is completely unbearable. I'm not sure which one's which.

"It's too bad Brianne couldn't make it," I say, managing to sound like I've risen from the crypts but my throat has yet to get the memo.

"Oh. Yeah..." replies Dylan, sounding almost surprised that my vocal cords still work. That's probably why he sounds surprised. Or maybe it's that I expressed missing Brianne at all, considering I hardly ever talk to her when the three of us hang out. He's probably wondering why we're even bothering to hang out. He's just going to spend the whole time being annoyed at me—

"Did you hear what I said?" asks Dylan.

"Uh, no. Sorry, spaced out," I say, trying to sound apologetic.

"It's all good. I just asked why Brianne couldn't make it."

"Her little brother didn't tell her he needed a ride until about twenty minutes ago."

"Oh."

"Sh-she didn't tell you about it?"

"No. We haven't talked in a couple days. Sucks for her brother to do that though."

"Yeah."

It's surprising she didn't text that info to everyone, I think to myself.

Not as surprising as Brianne considering you before Dylan, who she probably knows better than you, myself adds back.

Shut up.

I truly cannot imagine why Brianne didn't let Dylan know what was going on. Not only is she one of the most considerate people I've ever met, she and Dylan have known each other for a while. They always seem to have their own in-jokes, and conversations between the two can often last for hours if you just let them go at it. I've almost gotten through a full novel listening to them debating the legitimacy of decanonized *Galaxy Quarrels*. They're clearly close friends.

You will never be that close to Brianne, or anyone for that matter.

Shut.

Honestly, there's no need for that. I don't know why I bother. Being a constant nuisance to myself won't change anything. What does manage to change is our proximity to the haunted house. I can see some people forming a line a little bit ahead of us, which further supports my assessment. I check my phone to confirm the address, but there's no need. Our destination should be right around the corner.

"I think we found the place, more or less," I say while we join the line.

"Yep," he says, leaving nothing but a familiar silence behind.

I can't help but think the worst when conversation lulls like this.

Current example: *He probably just wants to get this over with as quickly as possible and would rather not waste time speaking with me.* Although I may be reading too much into it.

Ya think?

Not helpful.

It really wasn't. There's honestly no need for me rubbing my own incompetence in my face when it comes to this being social thing. I don't see my deranged habit stopping anytime soon though, so I let it drop. It's not like I have any choice in the matter.

This is always the worst, talking to people, I mean. Every time, it goes like this: I say something, they respond to the question and, if I'm lucky, ask another question back, which I answer, and then...nothing. There's nothing else to say, or at least, nothing else I can think to say. And it's clearly my fault. Other people seem to have no problem maintaining prolonged interaction without letting silence take over, but for me, it's one of the hardest things in existence. Sometimes I wonder to myself why I find it so difficult, but I don't have the heart to follow through with that answer. It's much easier to just accept that talking to people is hard. Why am I so hesitant to speak? I just am. Easy answer.

I'm downright impressed that Dylan is putting up with this. It can't be fun spending time with someone who has nothing to say. If I were him, I'm sure I'd hate it. Or maybe he does. He's currently gripping his wrist and half of his palm with his other hand, as if he's trying to give it a new pulse. That must be him trying to distract himself from how awful of a time he must be having. I'm certainly not helping him out by keeping my mouth shut. Don't get me wrong, I want to say something, but I know next to nothing about him or what he likes talking about. I comb through the memories of our minimal interactions in an attempt to come up with something, no matter how trivial.

Let's see...he likes video games, and uh, comics, I think? He and Brianne have talked about all that stuff ad nauseum. None of these things are my expertise. I'd just be parroting their own thoughts and opinions on those subjects. What do I do?

My mind's still drawing a blank, but I really don't want to continue the rest of this wait in silence. We still have some time to kill before we actually get inside and the only thing worse than a long silence is a silence that's happening only because of me. As people shuffle forward and we get closer to our goal by the step, I try to make a conversation happen again.

"So, you uh," I start to say, and as I do, he makes eye contact. It makes me forget what I was going to say for a second, but I recover the thought before there's too long of a pause, "ever been to a haunted house before?"

That's the best you can do?

Luckily, I don't have enough time to get even more down on myself before he responds.

"Yeah, once. Oh wait. Now that I think about it, that was just an escape room with a spooky theme. The group of people I went with didn't manage to get out in time, but we still had a blast all the same. What about you?"

"No, I've never been to one."

"Really? I wouldn't have expected that. You seem like the type of person who's into scary stuff."

"What makes you say that?" I ask. He's spot on; I've always had a taste for horror, but I can't figure out what made him think that. I've barely said a full sentence to the guy before this outing.

"Those books you always read."

Oh, right. Why did he bother to notice that?

Don't know, loser.

Can we not?

Whenever Brianne would drag me to a group hangout, I'd always bring a book. It always felt like I needed it. I've yet to regret bringing one. It's a lot easier to read than to bust your way into a conversation. Much more entertaining too.

"Usually," continues Dylan, "the covers I've seen you read look like they're horror-related, or suggesting a dark tone, at least. Am I wrong?"

"No, not at all. That's my preferred genre."

You have an easy connector. Don't screw it up.

"Uh, what kinds of books do you like to read?" I ask, as we shuffle forward along with the line. Dylan looks to the ground and starts gripping his wrist again. I panic.

Maybe he doesn't like to read. I shouldn't have assumed.

Sure shouldn't have, ass.

I attempt damage control.

"If you read, I mean. Do you read? Well of course you read—you're literate, haha...I meant like—if you read for like, for fun—"

"Hah. Jeez calm down. I got what you meant. Yes, I do read. For fun, that is. I like reading sci-fi."

"Oh...coOl." And my voice cracks. Great. I stare at the ground and try to avoid eye contact as much as human limitations will allow.

My chest hurts from how much I've managed to embarrass myself just now. If my face wasn't already red from the cold, I have no doubt it'd be shining bright by now. I'm genuinely at a loss for why Dylan is putting up with me. It can't be fun spending time with someone who can barely stammer a coherent sentence together. I try to keep myself from thinking about it too much by examining the house.

I'm kinda surprised the place looks as normal as it does, just your average two-story suburban house, built entirely of bricks except for the concrete-based porch. There's light coming from the windows on the first floor, but most of the second remains dark. It's all so average looking that the thought of anything paranormal happening there doesn't seem like a remote possibility. Even the surrounding houses have the spare carved pumpkin or two for next week's holiday, but not this place. Brianne must not have done much research when picking the house. Lucky for her that she couldn't make it, I guess. I have no doubt she would've been disappointed. Maybe the inside is where the terror really shines.

At this point, we're right at the front of the line. They have a young woman who looks not that much older than me at the entrance, letting people in one group at a time. Once she's finished ushering in the people in front of us, she turns back our direction and starts explaining things, going into this long spiel about how the house works. I start zoning out about thirty seconds in, but get the gist from half listening. Apparently, this place has some legit claims of a haunting or two in recent history, so Brianne wasn't that far off the mark with this place after all. However, to appeal to kids, the first floor is dedicated to the kind of cheesy, over-the-top schlock that is a horrifyingly inaccurate representation of what it means for something to be scary. That's not how she put it, but she might as well have. This wouldn't be a problem if we didn't have to apparently wait about twenty minutes to go to the second floor where the actual scares and suspense are supposed to be.

"With that out of the way," she says, "can we get your cell phones from the both of you?"

"Come again?" says Dylan, as he's rummaging through his wallet for the entry fee. I start to do the same.

"We're not going to do anything to them, I swear. We just don't want anyone taking pictures and posting them online. It would spoil the experience for anyone who's never come to the house before. Understand?" She addresses the question to both of us, but I look away the second her gaze moves toward me.

"I guess so," says Dylan, clearly not a fan of the idea. I'm less than thrilled as well. My phone is a safety net I can use to look busy or occupied, so no one can see how much I flail when I attempt social interaction. However, Dylan puts his in the box and the only thing worse than a social loser is an uncooperative social loser, so I do the same, being sure to pocket the headphones I still had plugged into it. Can't be too careful. We also hand over our cash while we're in the middle of unfavorable transactions. I'm not sure how I feel about relinquishing my cash for something as low stakes as this, but it's far too late to reconsider. After receiving ten bucks from both of us, the girl ushers us inside.

"Thank you. If there's an emergency and you need to get ahold of your phone, I'll be right here. And that's everything you need to enjoy our house. Have fun, you two!"

"Thank you," says Dylan with an inflection of enthusiasm. I murmur the same, minus the enthusiasm.

I don't exactly appreciate the emphasis she put on "you two," but I try not to dwell on it. Now that we're inside, I can see a small group of people at the stairs in the back of the house. Like the staff outside said, we'll have to wait a little, but it shouldn't be as bad as the first line. The grouping is still large enough that we might as well walk around the first floor for a bit before getting in line ourselves. I don't think I could take another long period of silence standing in place anyway. I walk into the first decorated room and look around.

Are you kidding me?

The room is fully lit and has only two boxes shoddily covered with cardboard paper. It would be generous to even call the place festive. There's a younger kid running around who shows the telltale signs of a sugar high. I feel bad for the couple watching him. I don't think they're the kid's parents, they look too young, so I imagine one of the two got stuck babysitting a little sibling. Makes me feel bad for Brianne all over again, even though there's nothing to be done about it now. I wish she was here.

Since there's time to kill, and we paid to get in, I walk up to one of the boxes and play along.

Gee, I wonder what they could be.

I stick my hand into the first box and feel around inside. The label says eyeballs, but I say grapes.

"What a joke."

"No kidding," says Dylan behind me.

I chuckle a bit and wonder if he intended that wordplay, although I don't have the guts to ask him.

Speaking of guts, I move on to the spaghetti—no wait...*linguine* guts—which gives Dylan room to join the party. He plunges his arm in and feels around the first box for a second and then turns to me.

"You think I'd get in trouble if I popped one of 'em in my mouth?" asks Dylan, "I'm kinda hungry."

"Do you have any idea how many hands have touched those 'eyeballs' tonight?"

"No, but good point."

I don't see him with a grape or an eyeball in his hand as we move to the next room, so I assume he took me seriously. Taking a look around, I'm too disappointed to be shocked.

We paid for this?

The room has a bunch of skeletons hanging from the ceiling. That's it. I don't see how even a kid could find this entertaining. They're not even the same kinds of skeletons. Cartoonish depictions are placed right next to real life models you might find in a science lab. When I walk past one of the more colorful looking specimens, it starts singing one of those stock holiday jingles. I hear a yelp behind me. I slowly turn around with what I think is a smug look on my face. I don't say a word, but my silence speaks volumes.

"Don't—" Dylan starts.

"Oh, I won't say anything, but I am *definitely* not going to forget that just happened."

"Ugh, just don't tell anyone, all right?" he asks with a smile.

It's funny how he thinks you know enough people willing to listen to your stupid gossip.

"I'll think about it," I say.

The third and final room before the now nonexistent line to the second floor is labeled "Haunted Maze," but I have trouble seeing how anyone could in good conscience call what's going on in this room either of those things. I stare at it in disbelief at how little effort was put into anything here.

"This maze is a line," I say.

"This maze is a line," repeats Dylan. We walk through the room with no other comments and wait by the second floor. No one comes down to show us up to the next floor.

"Guess they're busy up there," I say.

"Yeah." Three hours pass in the span of thirty seconds.

"Welp, I'm going to find the bathroom. I'll be right back," says Dylan.

Wow, he really hates spending time with you.

"Sounds good," I say. Dylan leaves, and I'm left to think, which is always super fun for me. Before I can think too long, I hear footsteps above me. People are heading back to the first floor. I move out of the way. The attendees head for the door outside but the attendant accompanying them stays behind. He sees me.

"Are you ready to head on up?" I cough to make extra sure my throat's clear.

"Well, technically yes but—"

"Ok. Then follow me." I freeze.

Speak up, idiot. Speak up. All you have to say is...

"I..."

"Hey, are you all right?" the guy asks, which seems like a reasonable question to me. From his viewpoint, he sees only a person participating in the haunted house acting weird for no obvious reason. But instead of being able to explain myself, a less rational part of my mind offers input.

Don't make a scene. Don't make a scene. Don't make a scene.

And for some reason, I listen.

"I'm fine."

"Ok. Just wanted to make sure." We start heading upstairs.

What are you doing? *Dylan's not gonna know where you went. Why are you such a moron?*

"It's fine," I mutter.

"What?"

"Nothing." That's what I try to convince myself. "It's nothing, It's fine, You're fine" are all things I try to tell myself to calm down and it never works. Every time in the past I can remember, the mantra devolves into a series of "don't don't don'ts" until I inevitably fail to cap a lid on my emotions.

As we walk up the stairs, I manage to maneuver myself in front of the guy before any fluid leaves eye sockets, so I'm in the clear in terms of social embarrassment. Assuming that I'm heading the right way and don't have to turn around. There are fewer situations I could conjure up in my head that I find more humiliating.

Why are you such an idiot? *Why can't you say things any basic human could cough up in their sleep? What the hell is wrong with you!*

I hate asking myself questions like that. They're designed to make tears flow more than they already have been. Thankfully I was right. We're headed to the end of the hall. I don't have to explain why I've been crying. The attendant goes along with the program he's likely been facilitating the entire night.

"Ok. This room has had multiple reports of paranormal activity in the recent past. I'm going to have you walk through the door. I'll close it behind you and will come back in a few minutes to let you know your time's up. Is that all right?" I manage to choke out a "yeah," which seems to satisfy him.

"Awesome. Happy haunting." I open the door and walk through.

The door shuts behind me, as promised. Once I hear the guy's footsteps recede into the distance, I try turning the knob. It's locked.

This is really unsafe. What if there was a fire? Or an earthquake? Or a gas leak? I'd be done for. I wipe my eyes with my sleeve.

The place is unlit and it looks like they removed any furniture that might've been in the room so people wouldn't trip on something and sue. The light from the hallway is still seeping through. It takes a couple minutes for my eyes to adjust. Once they do, I can make out the dimensions of the room pretty well. It turns out I was wrong. There is one thing in the back corner of the room. I walk toward it to get a closer look.

It's a mirror. A full-length one on a stand. There's nothing tricky or spooky about it from a first glance, but just to be sure, I inspect it from all sides. I even feel the stand for any minuscule hidden panels. Maybe the attic is supposed to function like a mini escape room with the haunting premise acting as a hook. Unfortunately, not. It appears to be just a mirror whose most notable quality is that you can use both sides of it to look at yourself in. Nothing about the apparatus is remotely spooky.

I stare at it for a minute, seeing what I can make out of the room in the mirror, but it doesn't hold my attention for long. I start pacing, but even that gets tiring.

I don't know how long they expect me to stand in a dark, empty room. It might at least be fun if someone were around to bounce complaints off of. I mean there's always myself, but I was referring to someone worth talking to.

Why couldn't I have just waited for Dylan to come back?

You're assuming he didn't ditch you. How generous.

I ignore that and wait for what feels like another minute before trying the door again. Still locked. Really, the whole setup might've been scary enough to distract me from my own thoughts if they put more effort into anything at all. You have to do more than turning off the lights. And even that aspect could use some work.

Honestly, they should've at least taped paper on the bottom door to block out the light. Kinda ruins the blackout effect if you can see almost everything anyway.

"Couldn't agree more."

The voice shocks me, especially since it sounded like it was coming from inside the room. I would've noticed if there was someone else in here with me by now. It not like there's a closet for another person to hide their presence. I survey the room, searching for a speaker. My eyes wander to where the mirror is to see another person standing there. Even though I can make out most of the room in the dim light, this person just looks like a shadow.

Where did she come from?

"I've always been here," she says, "you just haven't noticed before."

"Ok? Sure. Maybe you hid somewhere. I'll give you that."

"Oh, I wouldn't say I was hiding. Check the mirror and you might see what I mean."

I'm not entirely sure what she's getting at, but I oblige. As I move in front of the mirror, I don't like what I see, or what I don't see rather. I see everything that you would expect to find in a mirror, minus myself. I wave my arms in front of it. Nothing changes. I touch it just to confirm there's actually a mirror there. Feels smooth like glass. No, it's definitely a mirror. I was staring at my reflection just a minute ago. I can still see the rest of the room reflected in it. Why am I left out of the picture?

"I'll give you a hint if you want. You're not a vampire. You aren't cool enough to be a vampire. But you might have enough unwarranted angst to pull off the role."

Rude.

"Oh, come on. You know it's true."

"What's wrong with this mirror?" I ask.

She sighs with a dash of exasperation.

"Did you really not figure it out yet? You know, I always thought you were stupid, just not in that way."

"Who are you?"

She chuckles and shakes her head.

"Take a closer look. Ring any bells?"

I look her up and down. She's got brown hair and is wearing a hoodie with the sleeves rolled up that looks way too loose on her. She would probably look a lot taller if she didn't have that much of a slouch. If I didn't know any better, I would say—

"Ding ding ding! We have a winner! I am, in fact, you!" she says, the words drowning in enough insincere enthusiasm to make me cringe.

"That's not how my voice sounds."

"To you, anyway," she quips. "Do you ever bother to consider what other people hear when you speak? I guess not, since you hardly talk in the first place."

I am aware that generally your voice sounds different to other people than it does to yourself, but that doesn't mean I believe this girl. She might look like me, but she sure doesn't act like I do. It must be a body double, some expert they hired to profile people to act as their doppelgangers for a scare. That's the only explanation that makes sense.

But does that *even make sense? No, no it has to. What else could explain it?*

"Quit living in denial. You and I both know this cheap-ass place doesn't have the budget to pull this trick off," she says, while gesturing to her whole person, "If you want proof of who I am, who else would know the reason why you went months without talking four years ago?" Just getting baited to ask is bringing up uncomfortable memories, but I don't know what else to do other than quiz her.

"Fine. Why did I do that?" I ask, my voice barely above a whisper. She doesn't seem to care.

"Easy answer. It was just to see if people cared enough to ask. Sad, isn't it? Although, to be honest, I could've just said your birthday. No one you know even cares enough to know your fucking birthday. Or your name while we're on the subject of pointless things to know."

All right, I believe her. I don't really have much of a choice after that harassment. No one bothered to ask why I stopped talking. Even my parents didn't ask. It was so simple, so why did I bother doing that? But at the same time, if it was simple for someone to ask, why did no one bother to do so?

No. Stop thinking about it. I've beat myself up over that period of my life many times in the past, but hearing it out loud hurts even more. I'm used to dealing with this shit in my head, not standing right in front of me. This whole setup is pretty ridiculous. It's like some stupid horror story with an ending that probably wouldn't work in my favor. Unless I can think of a way out of this.

Now what would be stupid enough to work?

I look around the room and then my eyes settle on her. She's standing in front of the mirror, blocking it from my view entirely.

Is she trying to protect it? She did say that's where she came from. Maybe it's her lifeline. That's usually how this works in all the books, isn't it? The demon or whatever monster that's terrorizing people usually has an object their power comes from. If I destroy it then maybe she'll go away too...

She turns her back to me and heads to the mirror, putting her hand on the supposedly reflective surface.

"I know deep down you don't really think smashing that mirror will work," she says, tracing her index finger back and forth over it before clenching her hand into a fist, "and you're right."

She punches through it. Shards go flying and I cover my eyes. When I uncover them, I see scattered pieces on the floor, along with drops of blood. Her left arm. It's almost completely slick.

A thought crosses my mind that doesn't make any sense, but it crosses my mind regardless.

What if when she hurts herself...

I'm afraid to look, but the dread I feel is a compelling companion. No blood. All the same, just staring at some version of myself cut up like that puts me on edge even more than before. I rub my left arm to try calming down a bit, and it may have worked if I didn't have eyes to observe the state of my right limb. Wet, sticky, and cut open. Noticing the damage seems to force me to acknowledge the pain as well. It's not pleasant. But something about this nonsense still doesn't make any sense to me.

Why the right arm and not the left?

"It's a mirror. I came from the mirror. How else did you think it would work, dumbass?" I try ignoring her, but my mind keeps going to uncomfortable places. *Could she kill me?*

"I don't know. Have you ever tried to kill yourself?" she taunts.

"Coming from anyone else, I would consider that an invasive question, but no. Never." She strides toward me and I back away until I hit the wall.

She gets right in my face.

"Are you so sure about never?"

"Get away from me!" I shove her aside, but as I do, my left shoulder slams into the wall. The unexpected defiance of physics shocks me more than the actual pain.

"Equal and opposite, moron. What part of that do you still not understand?"

I ignore her and go back to the door, try the knob again. Still locked. I slam myself against the door. It doesn't budge. I try it again. Then again. My shoulder will probably bruise later, but the door remains in place.

Why isn't anyone coming?

"You heard that bozo walk away, didn't you? No one's waiting by the door to let you out. And anyway, I'd rather you stop. My shoulder is starting to get sore."

"Fuck off."

Although I hate admitting it, she's probably right. No one's on their way to help. I need to find a way out of here, but I'm running out of options. The door's locked and I'm not strong enough to bust it open. I take a deep breath.

Okay, here we go. Just do it.

I'm about to yell when I notice she's gotten in front of the door.

"What do you want now?" I ask.

"Really think about this carefully. You're smart enough to do that, aren't you? What were you going to do? Scream? Call for help? Let's look at it this way. You scream. People open the door. They see your arm all bloody and after realizing you're not part of the show, they ask you what happened. You tell them how this evil version of yourself broke the mirror, which caused your arm to spontaneously bleed. After all, you didn't break it. I did. But here's the thing. I'm not there. Well, I am there. Except there's only one person in the room. Maybe Dylan comes back to check on you just in time to see what a fucking *psychopath* you are! Can you handle being known as that freak who had a mental breakdow n at the world's friendliest haunted house? Sure, maybe your 'friends' stick around, but there will always be those thoughts in the back of their mind, like, 'What the fuck went wrong with her?' or 'Will she do it again?' Maybe even 'I better tread lightly. She might freak out on me.'"

This is such bullshit.

"Yes, you are," she says.

Shut up. Just shut up.

"Make me."

"I will."

"No, you won't. There's only one way to make me go away and if you do that, everyone will think you're crazy. Wait, let me rephrase that. Everyone will confirm that you are crazy. I mean, who the fuck talks to themselves as much as you do?"

Shut up.

"Why don't you try saying that out loud? Unless you finally admitted to yourself that you're the only one here after all, crazy."

I can tell she's trying to bait me, but I can't hold it in anymore.

"Who cares?"

"Huh? You, apparently. Can't you see my tears? I'm not the one with something to cry about." I do feel the tears falling down my face, but this isn't even close to the first time I've cried out of anger instead of sadness.

"Who cares what I think or what you think? None of it matters! Not one bit. The world keeps going on without me. What the hell does it matter what other people think of me? I'd rather be an alive crazy person than dead."

She pauses, like she's taken aback by my words. She makes eye contact with me and smiles like she just heard the funniest joke in her life. I never liked my smile.

"Oh no. No, no, no. You can*not* play that game with me. I know better. You care what people think. Why else would you shy away from talking to anyone? You barely even talk to your parents. When was the last time you said a word in class? Too afraid the other kids will bite your head off? You never go out and have fun, always cooped up in your room, reading novel after novel, as if that would give your life meaning."

"Not tonight," I protest, "I'm not doing that tonight."

"Please. You only took the headphones out of your ears and the books out of your hands because you thought the one person who took pity on you enough to call you their friend was expecting you to come. Of course, you had to keep up the appearance that you are a normal, functioning human being that is worthy of being classified as a person. At least for her. But deep down you know she hates you. Brianne just keeps you around so she can look like the better person in front of her real friends."

I want to argue, but her words cut deep. I *don't* think that...I don't think that. But even so, I can only think of one other person to counter her claim.

"Dylan..."

"Dylan? *Dylan*?" she says, trying to contain her laughter. "You must have a sick sense of humor. I was there. The fact that you managed a conversation for more than five seconds was a fluke. A miracle bestowed upon you that will never repeat itself. Before your little boon of a talking bug bit you on the ass tonight, that's what always happens. You've never had any trouble accepting you don't have any friends before. At least a speck knows it's an insignificant piece of the universe. What makes tonight any different to make you think you're more than something people secretly hate?"

I could answer her question, maybe retaliate against her insult, but no matter what I say, only venom would get spit back, I'm sure of it. According to her, nothing I've ever done has been worth anything. I wasn't lying when I told her I'd never thought of killing myself, but there were times when I would sit in my room and wonder if what I was doing mattered at all, or if I had screwed up somewhere along the way, choosing the paths that made the social, outgoing person that I could have been disappear from existence. What exactly am I supposed to say? This mirror replica of myself keeps insisting that I, as a person, am not worth anything. That no part of me is worth anythi—

Wait...that's it!

"What? You decided to off yourself after all? Plenty of shards on the floor. Take your pick," she says, bending down to pick up one of the pointier pieces. "I think I like this one the best." She slides one of the sharper edges back and forth over her right wrist and arm, harshly enough to leave a scratch, but not enough to break the skin.

The same area on my left arm tingles, but I'm over the cheap scares.

"You're not worth it," I say.

"Pardon?"

"You heard me. You're. Not. Worth it. This whole time, you've been telling me that I am this worthless piece of garbage that doesn't deserve anyone. Well, if you're right, then why the hell should I listen to that worthless piece of garbage? They'd have no idea what they're talking about. And if you're wrong, then you're just some asshole that no one in their right mind should listen to."

So shut the fuck up.

As I think that at her, I glare as hard as I can in her general direction. Her eyes go wide and then quickly move to the ground.

"You...you...argh!"

I can see something shift in her. She, no *it*, is beginning to warp out of shape. Into a poor imitation of me.

"You don't know what you're *fucking* talking about."

"I know that I don't care what you think anymore."

I walk up to it and slap its face as hard as I can. Part of me still expects that to sting on my own cheek, but it doesn't. It, on the other hand, groans in response. I see its left hand clench into a fist. As it moves to punch me, I intercept it, keeping my grip firm. The blood on its arm hasn't dried all the way. The fist inches toward my face a little, but not enough to actually hit me before I squeeze its arm as tight as humanly possible. If I didn't keep my nails trim, I'd be digging them into its skin.

"Didn't feel that one bit. I guess you're not me after all." I can't help but inflect a little smugness in my tone.

It answers through gritted teeth, as if trying to hold something in.

"I was, you *bitch*. You won't make it far in life without me!" Its voice sounds old and echoey now. Inhuman. "You don't have any idea how *disgusting* it looks to see some worthless, insolent creature try to grow a backbone. Who's going to hold you back from doing something stupid?"

"No one but myself. The same self that is happy to be alive and thrilled with the prospect of never having to deal with you for the rest of my long life."

It glares at me, eyes full of unrestricted fury. I never knew something had the capacity to hate me so much. I don't think I ever considered it worth the trouble before. Suddenly its gaze changes, as if it just realized how to turn the tables on me.

"I'll be closer than you think," it says, "If you think you are the only person I've ever been a part of, you are dead wrong, you stain of an existence."

The idea it poses does concern me, but I have no reason to believe anything it tells me anymore. Besides, even if what it says is true, I've got too much momentum to bother asking what it means.

"Your threats don't really scare me anymore, now that I know you're not me. Get the fuck out of here."

"Oh, I promise you it's not a threat."

It stumbles backward, as if having trouble standing on its legs. It's amazing how quickly the humanoid figure can shift into something impossible to classify as human. It starts moving its mouth but the movements don't match with the words it's saying anymore.

"You'll miss me. Just you wait."

"Don't hold your breath."

I blink and it's gone. There are no shards on the floor. They're all packed up tight in the mirror. I stare at myself. Move my arms, both of which are fine, upon closer inspection. Before I can decide whether I'm a lunatic after all or I just fought off the most fucked-up version of Satan, I hear a familiar voice coming from the other side of the door.

"Sophie? Are you in there?" It's Dylan.

"Yeah I'm here. Could you open the door? It's locked on my side." He does and I'm finally out.

"So, how was it up there? Is it worth my time to give it a go?"

"Not really."

He chuckles.

"That's kinda what I thought. Let's get out of here."

Not wasting any time, we head to the exit. I barely resist the urge to kick all the "eyeballs" and "guts" from their boxes onto the floor out of spite.

It's colder outside than it was when we first arrived. My hoodie is barely cutting it anymore. I roll down the sleeves in the hope of retaining some body heat. I feel like saying something, and for once, I have something in mind to say.

"Dylan?"

"What's up?"

"Thanks for going with me even though we're not all that close, but I uh..." *hope we can get to know each other better.*

"What are you talking about? Not close? I've always thought of us as friends."

What?

"Seriously?"

"Of course! I mean, you don't talk much, but when you do, it's always something really thoughtful. Sorry, I'm not that great at the talking thing myself."

I scoff. "You could've fooled me."

"No, for real! Do you have any idea how bad I felt spending most of the walk over barely talking at all? That was awful. If I was better at holding conversations together, I could've made things less awkward."

I can't believe what I'm hearing.

"That's not on you, it's on me for not talking. I mean, what about with Brianne? The two of you can talk for *hours*."

"Don't sell yourself short. It's not just Brianne. Sure, she has a lot to say sometimes, but you always keep an open ear to us talking when we all hang out. You always have a question or some sort of hypothetical to steer our conversation in a new direction. I see you smiling and chuckling to yourself whenever we manage to say something funny."

"My head's in a book the whole time. I'm not actually taking part."

"Yeah, you read a bunch. So what? You're always listening in. You wouldn't be there if we didn't want you to be and you'd leave if you didn't want to be there." Even though all of that stuff is nice of him to say, I'm starting to get aggravated. I know what my problems are and they shouldn't just be swept under the rug so I don't have to deal with them.

"But I never contribute to the *conversation*," I say.

"I'm not buying that. That product's got a...faulty label that needs... returning?"

"What?"

"Never mind. The point is that you totally contribute!"

"No, I don't."

"Yes, you do. Do you even remember why we decided to go to a haunted house in the first place?"

"Yeah. Brianne wanted to go."

"Because?"

"Because she..."

Actually, why did she want to go? I think back on the conversation. I remember it came up when Brianne and Dylan started talking about ghosts and Dylan said, "Brianne, you are not going to find a ghost by trying to exorcise one from your brother!"

"But he *has* to be possessed! He's just too normal. I wasn't like that as a kid. Clearly there's satanic sorcery at work. We need to get the evil out of him pronto!"

"I'm almost positive you would not be able to convince any priest that a child acting normal is cause for an exorcism. Hell, you'd be in danger of the guy exorcising *you* since you're so insistent about it."

"That might be fun."

"You don't mean that! Anyway..."

At this point I zoned out for a bit. The book was getting more interesting than the conversation, as it tends to do every now and then. I could still hear them discussing the issue, but I didn't tune back in until Brianne finally admitted her brother was in all likelihood not possessed by a ghost and/or demon as much as she'd like to believe.

"Well where *else* are we gonna find a ghost?"

"Haunted house," I said, while flipping to the next page, "that's a place they'd be." I don't even look at her while I said it. My face was glued to the book in an attempt to minimize my presence. For a good two seconds that had the magnitude of two hours in my mind, I could feel them staring at me. At the time, I thought they were bothered about me interrupting, but that's probably not what they were thinking at all.

"Hmm, yeah there might be some ghosts there. And it's even the right time of year," she said, while her brain siphoned energy from her boundless charisma and redirected the excess power into assessing the potential entertainment of the idea. "I'll have to look into it. If not we can always hit up the graveyard. They'll have ghosts aplenty!"

At the time, I really did believe that it was Brianne who came up with the idea. I downplayed my involvement so much that I remembered it wrong. After everything that happened tonight, part of me wishes we did just hit up the graveyard, but another part is happy to realize I'm not the nuisance I thought I was.

"Ok, I remember. You got me there."

"See? *See?*"

"That still doesn't prove anything."

"Then take my number. I don't know why I haven't given to you before now anyway." He holds up his screen so I can see the ten-digit number. I start typing it into "contacts."

"What will this prove, exactly?"

"Uh, it will prove you're less awkward than me by hanging out with you, obviously," he says with a fake snide tone.

"False. I am waaay more awkward than you will ever be. Just look at me."

"Then prove you are the most awkward being in the universe by hanging out with me!" Dylan takes a tone of fake aggression.

"Fine! Here's my number," I say with a similar tone. I send him a text.

"Thank you!"

"You're welcome!" As I say this, he looks down at his phone, my message probably just arriving.

"So, when do you wanna meet up?" he asks, fake aggression still in full force.

"I don't know yet. I'd prefer talking about it over the phone because talking about plans in real life weirds me out."

"Haha! Fool! I feel the same way. I wanted to do that from the beginning, but I was too awkward to say anything." Dylan looks way too pleased about achieving the upper hand through appearing more inept. I never realized what an absolute dork he was until now.

"I'm starting to think a lot of people feel this way about other people in general, but no one says anything because of these feelings!"

"Perhaps. I wouldn't know 'cause I only talk to like two people. This is getting too meta for my blood," says Dylan, slightly losing his tone of fake aggression.

"Fair enough. Now if you don't mind, I'm heading home because it's kind of late and I'm very cold," I say, a little sad to break off the conversation.

"See? Only a well-adjusted person could end a conversation so *flawlessly*. I would have struggled to get there for over twenty seconds that would've been painful for all parties involved. Goodnight. And I'll see you soon!"

"Night."

We part ways and I start walking in the direction of home. It's only after I walk a couple blocks that my brain starts processing what took place.

What just happened?

I've never done that before. I've never talked to someone for so long without overthinking every little thing. The conversation just *flowed*. I can't believe it even though it just happened. While I'm still dumbfounded, my phone gets a buzz. I haven't put in the number yet, but I know who it is.

"You busy this Saturday?"

Even though I just said it was even colder out, I feel kind of warm inside. And for once, it isn't because I feel embarrassed.

"Not at all."

EARL GREY AT THE CAFÉ DES FLEURS

J.D. Akins

A sleek black car pulled up outside a small café in the town of Chartres. A sign above the door proclaimed the place to be the Café des Fleurs. A young man stepped out from the back seat of the vehicle, waving for his driver to leave. The young man turned toward the café, the corner it occupied lit by the morning sunshine that poured over the tops of the buildings across the street. He was solemnly dressed and dour in appearance, as though he'd just come from a funeral. His black suit was ill-matched with the cheery disposition of the day. As the car he'd left trundled away down the cobblestone avenue, he straightened the end of his jacket and entered the café.

The inside of the Café des Fleurs was a host of overbearing sights, sounds, and smells. Behind the wooden counter to the left of the door, an older barista worked a squealing espresso machine, concocting several beverages at once with ease. Mugs and china clinked together on tables around the front room of the café, as the wrought-iron chairs scraped against the well-worn floorboards. Fine silverware shuffled over linen napkins and tablecloths. The Café des Fleurs was considered a place of refinement and elegance all throughout Chartres.

As the young gentleman passed by the counter, he placed down a small handful of pocket change and the barista instantly added another cup to the collection in her hands. She knew the young man's order perfectly. After the usual confirmatory nod from the barista, the gentleman made his way through the café, winding through the tables toward the sunroom in the back. Passing through the beautifully crafted French doors, he approached a larger table at the center of the solarium. Through the windows, he had a lovely view of the canal, its calm waters glittering with silver light. At the table, two people were already seated, in the middle of a vibrant discussion about the weather. The one seated opposite the doors, an older woman, stood and embraced the young man.

"Oh, dear Athos, it's good to see you." She kissed him on the cheek. "I do wish you'd dress a bit less drab, darling. You've got so little color already."

The young gentleman tried to brush her away.

"Madam Piaget. It's good to see you too," Athos said. He looked down at the older man, still seated, and nodded. "Monsieur Renoux."

The older man nodded back politely.

"Bennet," he said with his usual mix of congenial greeting and frank acceptance at the younger man's arrival.

Sitting at the farthest point on the circular table from the two older members of the group, Athos thought about the persistence of these weekly meetings and the strange composition of the party. This group of people called themselves "the League," after the work by the poet R.A. Kelton, "The League of September" (a personal favorite of Monsieur Renoux's). They met up at the Café des Fleurs every Sunday at quarter after nine for coffee and conversation: six people hailing from various occupations, all with their own reasons for being there and enjoying the company.

The older man, already seated, was Monsieur Charles Renoux, a locally famous philosopher and renowned author. His graying hair and bushy moustache gave him a rather scholarly look, one he likely cultivated. He often guided the League in tirades about poetry, plays, and music. However, Renoux's favorite topic to talk about was the weather. He could go on and on about weather forecasts and annual differences in the seasons. Most members of the group would rather he didn't carry on these lengthy conversations, but since he was one of the founders of the League, who was willing to stop him?

The other member who'd already arrived was Madam Lucille Piaget, formerly from Paris. She was the popular fashionista of the group, often feeling the need to give the other members of the party advice on their clothes and the latest trends. People in Chartres whispered that she had once been a famous member of the Parisian high society, blessed with grace and charm. These things tend to fade with age, and now she had to live vicariously through the younger members of the League. She was excitable and optimistic to a fault, known for hounding the members to join her for a variety of sporting games and parties. The only one to have taken her up on these offers was Monsieur Renoux.

Athos's ruminations were broken when Madam Piaget's sharp voice rang out to greet an arrival to the table.

"Oh, my sweet dear Ivy! Why on earth would you wear that again?" she yelped, jumping up from her seat.

Athos looked up to see the humble Ivy Walgrave, her yellow coat incredibly bright in contrast with the subtler colors of the café behind her. Ivy gave a quick smile to Athos. He tried to offer a smile in return, but was ineffective as Madam Piaget moved around Ivy and blocked her view of the young man.

"I mean, honestly, I wish you would wear a prettier dress than that." Piaget helped Ivy take off her coat. "That brown, in early May, in this part of the country? I wouldn't dare. Maybe something with floral print, perhaps. Hm, Charles?"

Renoux looked up from his tea to smile at the two women.

"I don't know enough on the subject to even hazard a guess."

Before Ivy could respond, the older woman spoke up again.

"Dear lord, you poets and philosophers are all the same. All smiles and excuses. Do you think the young lady would look better in flowers or in her brown...smock?"

"Pardon me, but I have excellent taste. Your question is inane. What does it matter what dress the girl wears?"

This exchange set the two bickering again, allowing Ivy to disentangle herself from Madam Piaget. She sat at the halfway point along the circle between the younger and older man, no doubt to distance herself from the preening of the fashionista.

Athos wasn't entirely sure how Ivy had been made a member of the League. He knew that she joined only shortly before himself, but beyond that he had very little to go on. In fact, Athos really didn't know much about the young woman at all. She lived nearby and rode her bike to the café every Sunday. Ivy worked in a flower shop, owned by her aunt with whom she lived. Athos wondered why she always seemed to show up only a few minutes after him. It was possible that the sight of his car in the streets of Chartres was her cue to leave home.

The next few minutes were marked by the arrival of Athos's espresso, as well as a hot chocolate for Ivy. The young man preferred coffee over tea. He thought the boiled leaf juice lacked flavor, and thus, any interest. Athos gingerly sipped his drink as the four engaged in small talk. Madam Piaget and Monsieur Renoux had a habit of taking up most of the space in the conversation, while Athos and Ivy were left to either nod along or comment politely when asked. It wasn't too long until another person darkened the doorstep of the Café des Fleurs, one of the final two members of the group.

Looking rather sporting in his blue jacket and well-tailored suit, Mister John Bailiwick was, in some circles, considered the epitome of the modern man. His combed and styled hair matched his dazzling personality that often made him the gossip of the League's women. He placed an order with the barista, Earl Grey with lemon, and made his way back to the table in the sunroom.

"Morning all!" he said, taking a seat next to Madam Piaget. "Athos, you're looking well. Getting out in the sun, I see!"

"Indeed, Mr. Bailiwick," Athos said, looking down at his half-drained coffee.

While Athos liked Bailiwick on principle, he found the man a little cloying during these meetings. He often wondered what the women saw in him. Sure, he was handsome, clever, and charming, but Athos couldn't quite get the appeal. Perhaps it was the fact that he worked as a solicitor and, on weekends, traveled to other parts of the continent. On these frequent trips, Bailiwick would meet interesting people, do interesting things, and see interesting wonders, just so he could relay these stories back to the League every Sunday.

With the addition of John Bailiwick, five of the six members of the League were in attendance by 9:15 on Sunday, the thirteenth of May.

Noticing this, Renoux spoke up.

"Why, does anybody know whether or not Miss Quinn will be joining us today?" he asked nobody in particular.

"I do hope she does," Piaget responded. "I always love her outfits. They have a divine sharpness to them."

A moment later in stepped a woman in her mid-thirties, her hair pulled into a no-nonsense bun. Horn-rimmed glasses framed her face. This woman's name was Minerva Quinn, and she was the sixth and final member of the League.

With her boots clacking on the wooden floor, she quickly placed an order for an herbal tea and strode back to the sunroom where the group was arranged. Athos had heard from Bailiwick that she worked in academia, as a librarian or professor at the Beauclair University outside the city. Unlike Piaget, Renoux, or even Bailiwick, Miss Quinn was a serious creature, one that Athos admired and feared in equal amounts.

"Good morning all," the woman addressed the group in her measured voice.

"Good morning to you as well, Minerva," Bailiwick said, standing. He pulled out the last chair at the table, seating Quinn between himself and Athos, forcing the younger man to shift his seat closer to where Ivy sat.

"Yes, yes, we all want a good morning," Renoux grumbled. He had an intellectual rivalry with Quinn. "Ms. Quinn, have you read the latest work by Kjartan Salvesen? It's simply breathtaking."

"I found it quite derivative," Quinn said, accepting her tea from the barista who'd brought it over. "His verse is empty and emotionless. His repetition obnoxious. It simply wasn't a good poem."

Renoux scoffed. In an effort to break the awkwardness of the ensuing silence, Madam Piaget spoke up.

"Well, I love that jacket dear," she said. "You must tell me where you got it!"

From that, the rest of the meeting carried on much as any other might. Polite conversation ranged around a wide variety of topics, from fashion to literature to film. During the couple hours they spent there, the League consumed vast quantities of coffee, tea, and croissants. While different members of the League went up to order, it was always Piaget or Bailiwick that insisted on paying for the group.

In the murky depths of conversation, Athos often found himself pretending to listen while, in reality, he was considering his own place at the table. He made sure he nodded accordingly and answered any questions posed directly to him, but his mind was turned inwards. All these people, excepting Ivy Walgrave and himself, were the original members of the League. Athos's grandfather, Doctor Horatio Bennet, had asked on his deathbed that Athos carry on his seat at the table of the informal society. The old man had practically raised Athos, and so the young gentleman had shown up precisely at 9:10 every Sunday at the Café des Fleurs. He didn't view himself as a member of the League, and felt as though he really didn't belong. Only loyalty to his grandfather brought him back every week.

Eventually, the sun had risen almost to its noonday height, and the members of the League had to disperse to their daily business. They gave their goodbyes, each one filtering out into the pleasant light of a beautiful day. Madam Piaget gave each one of their party a kiss on each cheek, a tradition she insisted on.

"Do try to look up a bit, dear," she said after pecking Athos's cheek. "Life isn't a funeral."

Athos simply nodded and mumbled a goodbye. He stood at the side of the street, waiting for his driver to arrive with the car. Ivy stepped out onto the curb after a tedious goodbye with Madam Piaget and Monsieur Renoux. The two would likely be in the café for another few hours, gossiping between themselves about the other members of the group.

Ivy unlocked her large silvery bicycle from the black metal lamppost out in front of the café and walked it over to where Athos stood. He turned as she approached and smiled, and she smiled back. Ivy stopped for a moment, holding her bike, looking as though she was going to say something. But, before Athos could ask what was on her mind, she mounted her bicycle and set off into the twisting streets of the city. The young man frowned. Unsure what to make of this, he started to wonder where his driver was with the car.

***

"Honestly, Charles, I have no idea why you're so infatuated with her work," Piaget said. "I mean, really? Her rhyme schemes are dry and her topics are so dreary."

"It's not about the topics," Renoux scoffed. "It's the importance of her work. Iris Bouchard was honestly one of the best American poets to come out of the nineteenth century."

Madam Piaget chuckled. The two elders of the group had been debating poetry for about thirty minutes to that point. Athos gave occasional interjections to the conversation, but was half-sure that Ivy had fallen asleep at the table. Miss Quinn was in Monaco for the week, on one of her common trips abroad, so the group was waiting only on the arrival of John Bailiwick. Luckily for the two youngest members of the League, he strode into the Café des Fleurs before Piaget or Renoux could continue their debate. Forgoing his usual Earl Grey with lemon, Mister Bailiwick quickly took off his jacket and slung it over a chair, sitting down.

"Everyone have their drinks?" Bailiwick looked at the assembled members of the party, speaking as though he were addressing a waiting crowd. "I assume none of you have read the news yet today?"

"I don't believe so, my good man." Renoux glanced at the others. "Is there something the matter?"

Bailiwick took a sharp breath.

"Last night, at about a quarter to midnight, at least by some reckonings, Crown Prince Bartholomew de Vanderstraeten was assassinated."

The others around the table gasped.

"They say that he was shot while taking brandy on the balcony of his mansion in the northern province."

"My word," Piaget murmured.

Ivy gave a sound like a small cough.

Athos simply sat in shocked silence.

"Why, do they know who shot him?" Renoux asked.

"They say it was the Populists that did him in," Bailiwick replied.

Everyone at the table knew about the Populists. They were a topic of conversation that came up from time to time, horribly macabre as they were. The Populists were a political group with ties to extremists who wished to overthrow the parliament and royal family of this fair country. Their dogma was built around their love for the country and the strength of the common folk, despite the fact that most people disliked their extreme, and sometimes violent, tactics.

"Those bloody bastards," Renoux growled. "They'll deserve whatever's coming for them!"

"Now, now Charles," Piaget put her hand on his shoulder. "Don't start anything you'll regret. Cool heads prevail, and whatnot."

The older woman's voice trembled as she spoke. She looked shaken to her core. The rest of the table was in silence. Eventually, a subdued conversation began. Ivy remained silent as the conversation began to grow slowly, like a fire, around her. Finally, she spoke up.

"So, what's going to happen?" she asked nobody in particular.

"I don't really know, my dear." Renoux sighed.

"Well, the parliament isn't just going to let it go," Athos said.

"What do you think they're going to do? Start a war?" Piaget asked.

"I was talking to some lads down by the shops, they say that's going before the parliament tomorrow morning," Bailiwick interjected.

"How would a bunch of kids working at shops know anything of national politics?" Renoux asked.

"It's simple. Lord Penrose of the western province takes his car from his manor around the bay to the local house of parliament every day. On his way, he stops down by the shops to glad-hand and buy some fresh produce. Some of the lads down there will ask him about government stuff."

"Well that's just bad politics, if you ask me! No tomnoddy off the street should be allowed to know what parliament is discussing!"

Madam Piaget piped up.

"I for one think it's nice that Lord Penrose still believes in talking with the people on the street. That's what keeps him so grounded."

The older woman turned and looked at Renoux.

"You're just angry you voted for that ghastly Lord Kendall last election."

Renoux grumbled something under his breath as Bailiwick spoke again.

"Let's not start drawing any conclusions yet. Whatever the parliament decide, we'll probably find out by next week."

***

One week later, the League sat around a radio in the Café des Fleurs, accompanied by the old barista and a couple other patrons of the café. A gentle rain fell on the glass ceiling of the solarium and rain clouds dimmed the usually bright room. It was conceivable that all citizens of Chartres, and even the whole country, were crowded into cafés and in their living rooms, eagerly awaiting the long-sought answer from the parliament concerning the death of the crown prince. All at once, the radio crackled to life and several members of the League stood up from their table in anticipation. The reedy voice of the radio announcer scratched from the small radio.

"Hello, Ladies and Gentlemen of Chartres, and welcome to a very special news report. Today is Sunday, June twenty-fifth, at exactly 9:35 in the morning," the speaker paused. "The leading story this morning: Parliament has finally reached a decision on the response to the assassination of Crown Prince Bartholomew de Vanderstraeten. Responsibility for the murder has been claimed by the extremist group the Populists, known for attacking monarchical and parliamentary government targets."

There was a second pause, longer than the first. Tension grew thick in the café.

"Parliament has decided to mount a full-scale search effort in the eastern mountains, a known location for Populist activity. No war has been declared."

A sigh of relief filled the room.

"While the country is in mourning, it is important to remember that the Populists are extremists, willing to go to great lengths to further their cause. Be vigilant of suspicious activity in your neighborhoods, and I repeat: No war has been declared."

***

A week later, war was declared.

The conflict wasn't started by the parliament, as they had decided against a full-on attack. The extremist group's numbers were too few and they were too far apart to present a clear military target, but the other side did not have such qualms. With the waving of flags and gunshots in the streets, the Populists promised to bring the monarchy to its knees before the common man.

In response, the government prepared for war itself. They called on all able-bodied men of loyal areas to sign up for military service. Luckily, neither Athos Bennet nor Monsieur Renoux were drafted. Renoux was an old man, not fit for the life of a soldier. Athos was the eldest male member of his family, and was thus exempt from service to take care of them. Only John Bailiwick of the League was called to service. He said his goodbyes to the group two days before he was to be deployed. The meeting had been a quiet one, mostly fond memories of shared experiences, like a wake in honor of a man who wasn't even dead. Madam Piaget wiped a small stream of tears away from her face.

"So, I guess this is it," Bailiwick said, standing.

"Write to us every day, dearest," Piaget said, letting out a little sob. "I'll miss you terribly."

Bailiwick chuckled and hugged her. He then turned and gave Renoux a firm handshake.

"You'll do your country good, lad," the older man said.

"I must admit, I never thought I'd be a soldier."

"Well, you just need to learn how."

Walking through the café, Bailiwick passed by Miss Quinn. He took her hand in his for a moment, the two sharing a soft exchange that the others couldn't quite hear. When he eventually stepped away, the rest of the League could've sworn they saw tears in the eyes of Minerva Quinn. Finally, Bailiwick turned to Athos and Ivy, who were standing near the café's door.

"Take care of yourselves," he said to them. Athos merely nodded, unsure of the correct way to respond.

"You do so too," Ivy said, tears forming in her eyes. Bailiwick smiled.

With that, Bailiwick turned around, giving one final wave to the League as he walked out

the door. With the goodbyes behind him, John Bailiwick went to war alone.

***

In total, the civil war lasted three years.

The next to leave the League during that time was Miss Quinn. Shortly following the departure of Bailiwick to the warfront, she took one last trip abroad. Piaget claimed that she settled somewhere in South America, but the rest of the group weren't so ready to believe this. Many sensational rumors claimed that the academic had joined up with the Populists, waving their flag high above her head. The League was disturbed by these stories, but never addressed them at any of their meetings.

A few months after that, Madam Piaget set out on a cross-country train, planning to visit family who lived in the southern province. The train had barely left the station when it was set upon by a group of Populists. Noticing her exquisite clothing and large collection of jewelry in the freight car, the rebels held her for ransom. Renoux tried to raise the money with the help of Athos and Ivy, but when the ransom wasn't paid in time, Piaget was killed.

The death of Madam Piaget shocked the remaining members of the League. Monsieur Renoux fell into a downward spiral after that, taking more brandy in his coffee than would normally be considered healthy. His demeanor took a sour turn, and the quality of his company dropped sharply. The last time Athos, Ivy, and Miss Quinn had seen Renoux, he was no longer the gruffly jovial older gentleman they had known all those years. Instead, he was an angry old codger, hissing and spitting like a feral tomcat, forgetting even the littlest things.

Eventually, it was only Athos and Ivy who met at the Café des Fleurs. The meetings grew more and more infrequent, months passing between them. One morning, almost one-and-a-half years into the war, Athos and Ivy met at the café for the last meeting of the League.

"My family has decided that it would be safer to wait out the war in Italy," Athos said. "We've a summer house in Florence."

The rebels were growing closer to Chartres by the day. Everyone was fleeing the city, fortifying their houses, or preparing to welcome the Populists with open arms.

"You're going?"

"Yes, I need to take care of my family."

"You'd just abandon this city?"

"It's for the best."

The young man stood and started to head toward the door. He paused when he heard Ivy say "Wait."

"What is it?" he asked.

Ivy moved around the table to where Athos stood.

"I've always been quiet. I'm not a very talkative person, that's all. I joined the League because Madam Piaget knew my father, before he passed. The woman thought she'd take me under her wing, give me the social graces needed for a young lady. But all I've learned is how selfish people can be. Piaget only wanted an attentive audience for her gossip. Renoux wanted people to argue with, so he could feel superior. Bailiwick wanted Miss Quinn, and Miss Quinn wanted nothing to do with us." Ivy paused. "But I don't know what you want. I've sat at this table every Sunday with you, and I don't have a clue who you are. We've never talked. Never had a conversation. Sure, you've been here at the League as much as I have, but I don't know you."

Athos stared at the young woman, surprised. Finally, he spoke.

"Come with me."

"Excuse me?"

"Come with me to Florence," he said. "You can bring your aunt as well. We both know this city isn't safe. You'll be safe in Italy; we can wait out the war."

The gentleman looked down, abashed. Ivy stepped over to him and raised his chin to meet her eyes.

"I would love to," she replied.

Two weeks later, Ivy Walgrave, her aunt, and the meager Bennet family left Chartres for Florence. In Italy, the two young people hit it off rather fantastically, taking in the sights of the continent. Athos's family rather disliked how much time he spent with the niece of a florist, but eventually ceded their complaints when Athos made clear that it was his money they were spending and that he could do as he pleased. They were in Florence for almost a year when Athos took Ivy to the Ponte Vecchio over the Arno River and knelt down beneath the central arch. She gasped as he produced a ring from his pocket.

"Now, I guess you know what I want," he said.

Ivy beamed down at him.

***

A few months after the war ended, Athos and Ivy Bennet returned to Chartres. They made a tour of the visit, finding all their favorite places that weren't destroyed in the retaking of the city from rebel control. They ended this trip at the Café des Fleurs. On Sunday, the seventeenth of August, Athos and Ivy entered the small café. Though there were bullet holes in the stonework and the lamppost outside was missing, the war had changed little. Upon entering the building, they heard someone ordering.

"Earl Grey with lemon, love," a voice called to the barista. Athos and Ivy immediately turned to look, but were disappointed to see a soldier stood there, unbuttoning the jacket of his uniform. The man noticed them staring.

"Can I help you?"

"Sorry," Athos began. "It's just we thought you were someone else."

"You're fine," the soldier said. "I'm Edward."

"Ah, I'm Athos Bennet, and this is my wife, Ivy."

"How do you do?" Ivy held out her hand in greeting.

"Athos and Ivy, you said?"

The couple glanced at each other and nodded to the soldier. The man laughed.

"Hah! Ol' Bailiwick used to talk about you both!" he turned back toward the sunroom, where Athos and Ivy could see a group of soldiers sitting around the League's old table.

"Don't you remember his stories about this café?" he asked his comrades. "And those people he talked with, the club? What was it called?"

"The Society, right?" one of the soldiers said.

"The League," Ivy offered.

"That was it!" Edward exclaimed.

"So, you know John Bailiwick?" Athos asked.

"He was a good man."

"Do you know where he is?" Ivy asked.

"Oh," one of the soldiers seated at the table said. "I guess you don't know then."

Athos and Ivy shook their heads.

"John Bailiwick died." The man paused and gestured to the other soldiers seated at the table. "He died saving us. We're all that's left of his squad."

"I'm sorry," Athos said, lacking for words.

"As I said, he was a good man," Edward said. "No doubt he lived a life as full as any."

The man looked wistfully for a moment before saying "Please, join us."

"We don't want to intrude," Athos said.

"No, no, it's fine, please."

The soldiers pulled up two more chairs. Athos and Ivy Bennet sat down with the four soldiers at the table of the League. They shared stories about John Bailiwick and the conversations that had happened at this historic table, the morning light shining in from the windows around them. When one of the men offered to get the couple some drinks, Athos was about to ask for an espresso when he stopped. The young man felt like a change.

"Earl Grey with lemon, please."

EVERY TEN YEARS

Kathryn Orwig

I get ten years. And then I die.

I don't remember the first time I died. Too young to understand more than colors and sounds, the feel of my mom's hand in mine. As soon as I came back, the clock started ticking down. I'd say in years, but that's false. When you only get ten, time measures in the breaths you exhale while running, the scrapes you gather on your knees and palms from inline skating, your mom's panicked eyes searching you head to toe as if she could stop the appointed time from coming again just by waving her hands around you in a high-pitched stream of verbal reminders to be careful, *oh so careful.*

No matter how many carefuls she's said, prayed, begged, time just kept passing by. Front teeth missing. Swallowing bubble gum whole, tree climbing, broken arm from tree climbing, ocean waves around my legs, hands, salt water in my mouth and white caps rushing over my head. Birthday cakes. Happy smiles for the cameras. Worried glances. Sidelong looks. As the candles increased. The ten years shortening.

A surprise trip. Anywhere I wanted to go right then and there.

"Just to the park."

"But you could go anywhere, pick a spot on the map, honey."

"I did. The park."

A sigh. Muttered words I didn't understand about "could be his last" and "he only wants to go play basketball."

"Let him be."

Tears held in check by a sharp inhale.

I thump the basketball harder. Louder. Drowning them out until the car engine turns over.

I turned twelve in the hospital. Days after I died. Everything hurt. To breathe. Move. Even to open my eyes, although my eyes are nowhere near my heart. Craning my head, I could just barely look. A new longer pink scar dived down my navel. Stitches zigzagging. Monitors beeping as IVs kept dripping.

"It's taking. Beating well."

"It hurts."

"He'll have another ten."

And then what? I want to demand. And then what?

But my mouth won't move to ask it.

Because I know I'll die again. But the next time I'll remember how it felt. The next time the pain won't be forgotten. Deep down I've always known, with the passage of time, with the years of my age, the knowledge gained shattering ignorant bliss, that the next time could be my last. If the heart doesn't take. If one isn't freely given at that time and place.

These next years aren't measured in bruises, basketball games, or waves, but in door slams, in music too loud, black clothes, a tattoo of a zipper top where the stitches scar ends. If Mom's not crying in worry, she's crying in frustration as she hurls at me—why can't I stop and just enjoy what I have? Here. Now. These ten years.

I don't tell her the pain is too close. Right under my skin. How my heart beats faster when there are no clocks around to watch the minutes turn over. But I don't need a clock ticking, leaves growing, maturing, falling, dying, to feel it like a bomb waiting to explode. Or a reminder it could go out like a candle flame. Barely a whisper between the here and now and infinity. My temporary heart held in my chest, caged by ribs, bone and muscle.

I don't tell her it's because I can't stand the quiet. Or being alone. Staying up all night, out long past dawn with people I call friends. Some are. Most aren't. But they tolerate me. Lend more habits to drown out the internal hissing, pumping, thinking of the inevitable as I try to drown the beating of this heart out, the feel of the thump thump thump that one day won't thum—Don't think about that. Less than two years. Drown it out.

Less than one. Just keep moving, moving, move—

This time feels different. The pain is still there. The darkness lingers at the edges of my vision. But it's slow, I'm slow. Perhaps it's because it's right before the official ten-year mark. I may even have my birthday at home this time if I'm counting the days right.

"Too much stress can do it. Lack of proper sleep and nutrition."

They are telling this to my mom. Reprimanding her.

"He can't keep going like this. The heart couldn't last. The next one..."

It's not her fault. I want to say. But my mouth is heavy, tongue thick.

It's mine.

I stopped measuring in hand-slapping-knee laughter, stars rising and falling, warmth on skin, snow seeping in boots. I stopped paying attention. Feeling. Because it hurt too much knowing joy when sorrow is right there too. Sitting there in the silence after a laugh, in the darkness of the night, waiting to slink in when I've had a moment alone. To realize I don't want to drown it all out. I don't want it to end. I want another ten years. And another. Until I'm old and gray and senile and laugh at everything. I want and want and want and I don't know if I'll have it.

If another heart will be found.

If it'll take.

If I'll get another morning waking up in a white-sheeted bed with the IV's drip-dropping and the monitors steadily beeping. Telling me I'm alive. That I've got another ten.

Because if I have another ten, it'll be filled with moments and memories. Some repeats. The taste of raspberries, sweet, bubbly. How sand sinks and gobbles up toes. The heavy silence in a waiting auditorium as the voices hush and the performance begins.

And many new moments. A ring on my finger when a loving hand slides into mine. The feel of the wind whipping past a height so high the birds soar below my feet. The taste of some fruit I've never heard of yet but I will come to try and exclaim its magnificence in being. These joyful things tinged in sorrow are bittersweet, enshrouded by end and beginning points of when I was reborn and when I'll die once more. The not knowing if I'll get another ten. The hurt and hunger because I do. I want it. I want *it*. Another and another. That painful truth sits in my chest thudding. Like a bomb.

Like a new lease on life.
I open my eyes,
And smile at the next ten.
Before I have to die,
I know I want to
Live.

THE BENDING OF REEDS

Kathryn Orwig

She clutches her bundled baby to her milking breast. Her light eyes dart from man to man steadily making their way through the narrow streets. Their white pants, bare chests, and wrapped headdresses glisten harshly in the soon-to-be burning sun. Sweat beads and rolls down her spine.

Back pressed to the wall, she clings to the shadows. She thought she had left early enough, yet the wails break with the dawn. Screams multiply as each piece of red laces the sky; like a mirror, the sky glistens.

She sucks in a breath.

As if her feet know something she doesn't, they move to go, sending pebbles rolling under her bare toes. Her heart beats faster, thudding against her chest so hard she's afraid her bundle will hear, wake, and give a cry—a fate worse than death. She must keep going.

The White Guards disappear around a corner. Their shouts echo, matched by the screams, but unable to drown them out no matter how loudly *they* follow orders.

She runs.

Sand burns her feet. Shadows cool her skin. Sun flares along her face. She needs the light to stop its path in the sky. Please keep me hidden. But it won't, not for her.

A piece of white fabric skids into view.

She tucks and hides in a door frame. Everything scatters for one blindingly still moment as the shadows bend around her body and the footsteps draw near and the sun keeps rising—

"No! No!" Another woman's screams jolt the White Guard away. The words turn into noise without form. There is no known tongue which can describe that sound.

She slides around a barrel without looking. She knows. Even the wind can't take away the smell, not for days; even the darkness cannot keep hidden what was done for long.

The coarse fabric stirs in her hands. Her grip tightens out of fear. Her feet barely touch the ground. The screams around her raise in pitch and die in throats. Her own breath rasps out of her body in shaky gulps.

"There! One is running!" a White Guard cries. The shout is given. It can't be taken back.

She whips her head around at the sound. Lips parting, wishing to scream, but all she can do is suck in the next breath. And the next, and the next. She ducks into shadow as they march into the light, their scythes still wet, their tread unshaken. Her legs whistle in pain, throbbing. She pushes harder. Rounding corners and diving through darkness and streams of sunlight. The mud bricks lessen, houses lay unfinished in the baking sun. The shouts are never far behind.

She crouches between low half-finished walls; the dried mortar scrapes her palms and arms. She fits her child between her chest and knees. Covering a hand over her own mouth, she tries to breathe the thick air. Slowly. Clamping her teeth to keep them from clacking—

"Where did she go?" Their tongue sharp, loud. Vowels dropping.

"Check there," a White Guard voices so close she can feel his body stir the air above her. She closes her eyes, lips moving silently—

The feet slap loudly. Quieter. Gone.

Fingers grip rocks as hands clutch undyed fabric. She pulls herself over the ledge and leaps down. Her ankles threaten to bend, but she keeps moving. Sweat coats her skin like a second sticky tunic. Her hair stays plastered to her face, but she will not move to wipe her brow. She can't afford to now.

Pebbles and sand turn to hard-packed earth. Brush grows waist-high, then chest, until it blocks out the sun's rays. Moist soil soothes her feet. When the cool waters of the rushing river wet her toes, she stops running.

A man watches the woman. He tilts his head as she claws, tearing the bushes for something she's dropped? Lost?

A sharp command cuts the still river air around them. The woman looks up as if caught in the gaze of a predator. Her movements quicken, torn reeds sail through the air until...

Tightly weaved rushes grace her searching fingertips. She grips and turns over the only thing she's had time to make, a palm woven basket. Coated in tar and rubbed smooth, it is sealed from the river's grasping touch. She hopes. She places it at her feet. Bending down, water soaks up her dress. The fabric swirls around her ankles. She barely feels the touch of rough wool on skin, as her eyes focus on the bundle in her arms. Slowly, she lowers her baby from her breast.

A small cry arises from the fabric. She moves a swath away and reveals eyes and short hair. Fingers reaching to curl around her hand.

For a moment she's still, and with eyes locked on the child, she doesn't see anything else. Especially not the man watching. She's young, barely as old as him. Golden hair against a skin tanned by heat that hasn't softened the ice in her eyes. If anything, the man thinks, her eyes burn with a flame as if the sky were falling.

Another shout.

As the woman scans the forest, she lurches deeper into the water, the basket skidding the short waves beside her. She turns and speaks, with a last touch to the child's forehead.

"River, take him from here, take him somewhere where he will be safe." The lilting cadence of her tongue is not his people's language. Soft. "God of my fathers, protect him."

With tears coating her cheeks, she covers the basket. The sobs don't have a moment to escape before another shout is given. With a last push, she sends the basket into the currents. He expects her to run away. But she doesn't race back into the trees. Instead, she follows the basket with her very steps. Over rocks she edges closer to the man, and he doesn't move to hide, nor does he speak. Even if he did, he doubts she would hear him as she's focused solely on the next part of that river. On that basket dipping out of sight in the next swell, and rising once more. Under again!

A yell causes her to still behind a tree. The shadows hide her well. So well he would never have seen her there, if he hadn't watched her melt into the bark.

The basket draws nearer, if he doesn't reach out it'll keep swirling downstream. Toward rapids. Beyond her sight and footfalls.

The man steps out of the reeds, he grips the basket and brings it closer until it floats at his knees. He removes the top and stares at the child. It has her light eyes but dark hair. Its skin, soft and smooth, wrinkled with the newness of flesh. It isn't ill, nor deformed. He frowns at it. Why did she cast it into the river? The child reaches for his hands wrapped around the basket, and curls its fingers around the man's thumb. The man feels warmth spread from his chest to his lips—

"What are you doing?" A screech; more sound than spoken syllables.

The man looks up. Smile wrong now. The woman is *hissing* those words at him. He steps back as she races to the basket, her eyes darting to the forest, then to the water.

"Put him back," she hisses, closer, ice eyes glancing behind her, to him, to the streams swirling past the basket. Back again, as if she can't look at one thing for too long. Hands reaching for the child.

"This is madness, why are you sending the child down the river?" he retorts.

"Are you mad?" Her words should injure his pride, but her tone is filled with disbelief. He wants to assure her he isn't. Yet, she cuts faster than him.

"Do you know nothing of this...this?" She searches for the words in his tongue as she lunges for the basket. He swirls it from her grasp. "This land?"

She jerks out and grips his arm, hard, stronger than he thought her capable of. Stopping him from spinning the child's basket from her again. Her eyes pierce with the question.

"I know this land more than you do; I can assure you of that." Who is she to accuse him of ignorance?

"Then you would know to let him go—"

"A child belongs at its mother's breast. Not floating down a river." The man picks the child up and cradles him, preparing to hand the infant back to her.

"You don't know anything. The emperor!" She grips his forearms, nails digging in, unable to speak another word. Her eyes dart back to the trees.

"The emperor? What crime could your child have committed?"

"Every nine years any son born is killed and thrown to the water beasts." Her eyes change, harsh ice to something almost hallowed. "My husband...he grew ill, and wanted... I tried to convince him...he got to see his face before he passed." She takes a breath, steadying her trembling, thin arms. Her eyes focus once more on him, lose the empty quality as he watches another emotion inches from his face: fear. "Please," her grip tightens on his flesh, burning him, "my son must go if he has any chance to live. He can grow up, far from here, *safe*." She grips the man's white fabric shirt, her fingers boney and sharp. He wouldn't be surprised to find holes punctured. "There's a city not far, someone will find him."

"The river won't keep him safe. The current, the animals—" He insists but even he can hear how weak his voice has become in the wake of her plea.

"But he'll be *alive*." Her gaze hardens. She believes this. "Please. Give me my child." She holds her hands out for the boy. "Let the water take him."

The man swallows, looks from her to the child. Her searching eyes, hoping. The child nestled in his arms is almost asleep.

A sound he has never heard before, singing? No, crying, but something worse...Women wailing. He stills. Listening.

She takes the opportunity, hands slide under his and the fabric shifts. His body angles to transfer the weight. But if he gives the child over, his hands will be light while hers will be burdened with blood. He holds tight and settles his heels further into the mud.

But she presses nearer. Placing a feather-light kiss to her son's head, she glides her hand down his face in a move so smooth and well-practiced, he would have thought she'd done this all her life. Instead of the weeks, the hours she's had with him.

The baby boy laughs at her touch and breaks into a smile so happy. The man stills, watching, but not a part of them.

"Please, let him live free, far from the emperor who would have him killed." She speaks, but doesn't need to meet his gaze for the words to nettle his heart. *Is it better to let the child go?*

The man looks at the sky, wondering if her God listened. He must have, because he feels his fingers loosen of their own volition.

"You caught her!" A voice cheers.

The woman sucks in a breath, she steps closer, hiding behind him out of instinct. Like the bark of a tree. Yet he can't hide her.

He breathes out, his spine stiff and formal with each snap of the reeds murdered as the White Guard stalks closer.

"Well done, Your Highness," the White Guard utters, "your father assured your capabilities with great wisdom."

He feels the woman still against him. The air trapped in her lungs as her breath doesn't cross his skin. The man doesn't want to look at her, but like her refusal to look away from the basket cutting downstream, he opens his eyes...

...To find a look so gutted, it is as if he himself cut down her child. Her cheeks sink, pale, mouth hanging open, but in her eyes...he sees his own image reflected in those deathly still mirrors of water and light. He almost flinches back.

Tearing up, turning red, threatening to gush, her lips tremble in a cry so silent her breath barely whispers against his cheek.

"E-emper-peror?" Her head shakes no, please say no. Please...no?

He barely can make himself incline his chin. Yes.

Her hands, wrapped so lovingly around his forearms, fall away. Where her warmth touched, seared ice blocks remain as the heated air drifts across the hairs on his wrist cooler than her flesh.

"What have I done?"

He winces, as if the words were screamed at him, although they are scarcely spoken past her lips. Tears streak her face as the screams get trapped in her throat and she can't do anything but look at him—*holding* her *son*—with those eyes.

Those frozen, raw eyes.

"Kneel before your emperor!" the guard barks, striking her down before giving her a chance to obey. She plops into the water at their feet. Dress soaking up, filling with more than her tears. She doesn't move to rise, but just lifts her chin to stare at the bundle in his arms. She'll watch her child die; she owes her son that much.

Even though slaves are not allowed to look up.

"The child, your Highness," The guard holds out a hand. The man looks at the hand, caked with red. At the curved blade tucked against the tunic, droplets coating the fabric. The starkness of red on white. "You've done your duty, allow me to do mine for you."

The woman inhales too sharply. The guard hears her and turns to strike again. The woman braces, but doesn't move to fight or dodge. As if he was the one to have fallen into the cold water, he understands why.

The child coos, squirming in his grip, reaching upward to the bright sky.

"You will not strike her." He speaks over the rushing river and wails floating on the wind.

"Sir? The child is a—"

"The child is mine. The woman was simply returning him to me." He meets the guard's eyes, pointed. The woman looks up at the emperor. Her gaze is full of questions, but one burning one rises above the others. *What are you doing?*

The guard's eyebrows raise, almost suspicious. "Then why was she running?"

"Would you have believed her?" His clipped words shut the White Guard's mouth. He steps back from the woman.

The emperor offers a hand to her. She looks at it. Doesn't wish to take it, but can't refuse openly. She slides her palm against his and rises from the river. Water dripping off her elbows and down her hands as she stands at his side.

"And the woman, sir? What would you like done with her now?"

He feels her tense beside him. Her child is safe. But she is far from that. And she will never be safe again...

"She'll be coming with me." He gestures to his boat and goes to take her arm. She flinches back. Stabbing slits his chest, although no one has made the cut. Her eyes speak for her.

He tries to convey as well as she does with her gaze. He must have done enough, because she gets into the boat and sits. "Not another word," he whispers in her language, stepping into the hull. Those three words surprise her more than anything else he could have said. He turns to face his guard. "Your emperor has spoken."

Again, the woman's eyes snap to him for a brief moment, but he does not meet her gaze. He can't, not now.

"Master." The guard bows low and turns to fulfill his orders, he has a quota to meet.

Only once the reeds still, and the last shouts turn into wails, does he meet her unflinching gaze. She reaches for the heavy bundle in his arms.

"My son—"

"Not yet," he hisses low, scanning the banks, "Emperors do not go unseen." Using one arm he pushes them into the current, guiding them downstream with a hand on the wooden pole. The other wraps around her child, as if it was his own.

"You speak my tongue?"

"A ruler should know his people's languages, should he not?" the man says low, watching the reeds bend.

"I am not one of 'your people'."

That brings his attention to her. "You are now."

Her eyes never leave her son. Never leave him—boring holes where her fingers had clawed, had touched, had *asked*.

Faster than he would like, they arrive at the palace floodgates, sailing into the shallow pools. As the shadows cross the boat, the woman gazes up. Stunned, her mouth drops open. Curious unbounded delight flickers across her face as her eyes drink in the silk curtains, marble pillars arching overhead, and colorful tiled floors. For a moment, he sees softness in her features. Long-stemmed plants hide their arrival, but not for a moment longer.

Servants appear, silent, but ready at the sides. He curses under his breath. He can't hide the bundle in his arms, or the woman sitting in his boat. His hands sink with the weight.

As his wife saunters from the courtyard to the edge of the pool, he helps the woman down from the ship, aware of the moment his wife takes in the sight—her steps slow. When he meets her gaze, he can feel the words she wishes to hurl at him. He knows. He promised her the world, his world, his life, and heart—and here he was bringing home another woman and her child. "Who is this, *husband?*" Her voice rings at the end, higher.

"The mother of my son," he says, loud enough that the servants can hear. "She'll be staying with us."

Her lips part, she shuts them. A moment, the gesture is repeated. And then, "How long?"

"As long as I say. *Wife.*"

She purses her lips, but her look sharpens on the young girl. And she is a girl, standing beside him, he notes the difference clearly between them. One raised from birth to be a empress. The other barely comes up to his shoulder. Hunched. Eyes lowered.

"She's missing shoes."

They all look down—the girl is already staring at the floor—to see how accurate the wife's statement is.

"I'll get your...*guest* some things." His wife turns and leaves, her steps measured and no quicker than before, although he notices how her soles tread heavily.

"Come," he says sharply, solidifying his decision. The young woman follows close behind him through the windy halls and open arches, her toes practically on his heels. He knows whose fault this really is. And it's not hers.

Servants pass them by, pitchers carried, floors scrubbed—they step past them all. Everyone bows low. The woman watches this, how their eyes never leave the ground. How they stare after her, but not him. If she had known he was the emperor...she would never have taken his arm. Never spoken so sharply to him. An interrupting tongue to a royal is lashes, what is a scolding tongue's price?

They stop at a door. The emperor opens it and steps aside for her to pass. She does so, slowly, her demeanor guided by mistrust. What does she have to go on? He lied to her from the moment he picked up her child.

Open light floods the room, curtains blow in the faint breeze, and the limestone glistens as the town layers and stacks outside the window. A bed, already made, stands against a wall. Baskets fill the room, while counters and shelves line the mud bricks.

She stares at it all, and reaches a hand out to touch the silks on the bed. But she won't meet his eyes. Those blue eyes won't tear from the floorboards, just like one of his servants. But that's what she is, isn't she? No, less than that, a slave. What has he done? He saved her child and herself, angered his wife, and she...she won't even look at him.

"I hope it is to your satisfaction." The edge in his voice doesn't bring her gaze up like it would have on the banks of the river.

"It's more than I ever could have dreamed, my emperor." But the words lack warmth or curses. Hollow. It hangs between them. She spoke to him with passion, with fear, she hadn't known who he was then, but she does now.

"Your wife...she didn't seem happy...I—we..."

"I'll explain to her what happened. But everyone else must think this is my son." He steps closer until she finally looks up. He holds her gaze, "Everyone." She nods. "I promise you'll be safe here, as long as you follow this single request."

"You mean order?" For a moment, that ice hardens. Then he watches her shrink in, remembering who she is talking to. Curving into her place, melting to find the floor, she barely speaks, "I understand, emperor of Egyen."

"This is not something you understand, but rather something you must ingrain into your every move and thought." He steps closer still. "No one can know. If someone, *anyone*, finds out, I will not be able to save your son again."

He offers the child to her.

Reaching immediately, hands sliding, for a brief moment that heat she radiates touches him—but doesn't sear or scorch. Only warms.

As she takes her baby from his arms, she matches his gaze, blink for slow blink. But he doesn't know what that look conveys. Fear? Resignation? Does she think this fate is worse than death?

"He'll be taught as a prince," the words rush out of him, "as soon as he is old enough, he'll spend his days with me. But at night he can sleep here."

She nods, in disbelief, it's more than she could have ever asked for. He risked his word, his law, for her and her son. Her son will be raised as a prince. But what will he demand in exchange? She knows...she can't hope... she has nothing else to give...

He waits. There's one last thing. When will he see something besides fear and mistrust in her eyes? When will he be someone other than the emperor she hates?

"He may call you mother. And I father. But he can never learn of his true father."

Silence. Her mouth parts for a moment, "But—"

"This is how it must be."

"I'll do anything to keep him safe." She places her son on the bed. He notes it as uncharacteristic. Frowning, he tilts his head to the side, waiting. With a breath out, she touches the strands holding her dress tied. "Anything that is required." The dress falls and the fabric pools at her feet with a heavy thud, drops of water slinking along the tiles.

He closes the door and steps to her, bending down he picks up her dress and places it back on her shoulders.

"Anything of that sort...is not required." He ties the strings. Her eyes search his, surprised that there is no trace of lust. "Then my wife really would geld me." He can't help but smile.

One she returns, fleetingly. Until she meets his gaze and once again it dies. "I have nothing else I can give to you."

"Give your son all the happiness you wished the river would have given him. That is all I ask of you."

He goes to step away. But she grips his hand, turning him back to face her. "He was in your arms, steps away from...it was your order. Your law. Your *right* to hand him over."

He steps closer. His gaze lands on her bruised cheek, even without touching her he caused the mark on her face. His name. His orders. His right by birth.

"I do not wish to be the emperor, *the man*, you saw on that river bank."

He turns and opens the door.

"Your Majesty," she calls. "I don't see that man now," she says, holding his gaze, steady. She believes this.

"Neither do I. Which is why," his gaze flicks to the window, "I have a council to gather, a law to change," He meets her eyes, "and some guards to position elsewhere." He steps out and as he closes the door, he glances back once over his shoulder to see her cradling her son to her breast.

STAR GIRL AND THE MARBLE ROLLER

Kathryn Orwig

FIRST APPEARED IN THE *CAFÉ SHAPIRO ANTHOLOGY* 2017, AND THE *RESIDENTIAL COLLEGE ALUMNI JOURNAL*, 3RD EDITION, 2019

Fredrick had an obsession with marbles. Ever since he could pinch one between his chubby little fingers, he had rolled them, slobbered on them (he was three then, and, as he says, who among us has not sucked on a marble at some point?), and even swallowed one once. He hadn't swallowed it because he thought it was food, like his mother insisted. He had swallowed it because he had seen the world through the cat's eye and thought that if he could take in the whole world in one bite, then it would dissolve inside of him and fill him with the deepest oceans, wildest forests and tallest mountains. But his mother never understood this and all that had happened was that the marble came out later in a fit of beets, carrots, and lettuces from the night before.

On the morning of his sixth birthday, Fredrick lay on the smooth, well-worn floorboards of his bedroom. His stomach pressed firmly against the ground, his dark brown hair swept to the side, and his sharp hazel eyes watched the marbles in front of him. They rolled along the miniscule cracks between floorboards, only to stop a few feet away in dips only marble rollers could see. His parents had given him a new batch of marbles to entertain himself with that morning, while they set up his party downstairs. He could hear their voices and even a few surprised bouts of laughter. It had been many months since Fredrick had heard his parents laugh together.

More marbles clinked in his bulging pocket. Fredrick absentmindedly fingered them, like one would a rosary. First feeling one whole, cool marble, then letting it slide through his fingers, warm from his touch, and then the next one. He liked the sound they made, a soft clink muffled by his pocket. He considered rolling three or four marbles in his hands like one would to start a fire (but slower of course), an absolute pleasure. Or holding a handful of marbles in one hand, only to drop them against one another, fast, and then slowly to hear that sharp clack sound. They were smooth, soft and so lightweight, as if they were filled with air instead of marble ingredients. He couldn't tell by feel which type of marble each one was, and this gave him a certain satisfaction when he did guess right after pulling one out of his pocket. Fredrick didn't have a favorite color of marble; the pattern was more important.

He was the best shooter of shooter marbles in his class, and the highlight every day at recess, in a corner on the black pavement of the basketball courts, was trying to see how many marbles he could make burst outwards like a small star explosion. And whenever they played the circle marble game—no matter how much Fredrick might want the runaway marbles—he always played for friendlies and never keepsies; he couldn't risk losing his own collection. He loved trying to come up with the best angle on the circle to knock two or three marbles outside the chalk-drawn line. It was even luckier if the shooter marble trundled out too.

Fredrick knew all the types of marbles. Clearies were made of one color, a clear marble glowing orange, fluorescent pink, bubbling blue—he liked those a great deal. Cat's eyes, which had a distinct three-color swirl, were some of his favorites. He was always torn the most, though, between loving Micas—marbles that shone so brightly in the sunlight they glittered—and Sulphide marbles—clear with silvery figures in them. Micas were rare and beautiful, but the figures captured Fredrick's attention. He wondered if they lived in there happily, or if they were trapped souls who'd been tricked into staying in the small glass bead. He figured some genie was behind making Sulphides. He still had yet to prove his theory though. He had one marble that he imagined was what his sister would have looked like.

She was silver, of course, small and dainty in the glass world. If he stared at the marble hard enough, he could see that she wore a little dress and a ribbon in her hair. Fredrick could not make out if she was smiling or frowning, and her hand was always kept outstretched, palm up. Was she inviting him to come to her world, or demanding a payment of some sort? The flecks in the marble behind her looked like stars. She even looked fragile, which is the way one ought to look after being a Star Girl, Fredrick always thought. A Star Girl, that was what he had overheard his aunt tell his mother on the day they buried his little sister's body.

Fredrick had wandered up to his room on the second floor of their two-story house while his mother and aunt talked in the kitchen. He knew they wouldn't say anything important if he was around. But they didn't know that if he lay on his stomach and looked down through the vent in his floorboards he could see into the kitchen below and hear every word they said. His aunt poured his mother more tea from the blue, yellow, and white Polish pottery pot, but his mother didn't move to take it. She just sat in the wooden chair, with her hands clasped tightly together over her stomach and her red-rimmed eyes locked on something far away.

"Clarissa...Clary," his aunt started.

"She didn't even make it to morning." His mother shot her hands to her mouth to keep the cries in.

His aunt got up and put her long thin arms around his mother's plump body, drawing sister patterns on his mother's back. Fredrick always imagined that only sisters could read the patterns their hands made. "She's a star girl, Clarissa, she's now glittering and shining with them all."

The girl in the glass marble was precisely that. The Star Girl.

Plates clattered downstairs followed by a muffled curse from his mother. A thought occurred to Fredrick. If the Star Girl was in the stars, then she could only see the world at night. And if she could only see the world at night, then she did not know what the world looked like by day. Fredrick got up from his bedroom floor and clutched Star Girl in his hand tightly. He ran from his room, down the stairs, and out into the living room, through the kitchen where his mother was picking up broken shards, and finally to the slider door. He pushed the door open and holding the marble up exclaimed, "See, Star Girl, look at all the flowers in the morning sunshine."

Water plopped on Fredrick's hand. He squinted at the sky. Dark clouds lumbered overhead and rain was just starting to drop steadily on the flowers in the garden, on the patio set where his party was to take place, and in the small blue pool they had just set up the night before. The little water toys careened and shook in the growing torrents from the sky, all about to capsize at any moment. It was so dark it barely differed from the light of night. Fredrick pursed his lips and looked up at the clouds and then back to the very wet (and getting wetter) yard. Star Girl rolled in his hand and settled next to the droplets of water. Fredrick's face started to fall as sadness crawled up his throat. He wondered if Star Girl was disappointed in him for not showing her the sun. He was now sure her face held the sternest frown. But then a drop of rain landed on her glass home and turned the world inside her marble upside down, and for the briefest of moments Fredrick saw her smile magnified.

The water slid and curved around the glass sphere, melting into the other droplets converging in his palm. Fredrick smiled, and as he raced out the door, he held Star Girl high in his fingers. High in the pale, rainy morning light.

"Look, Star Girl! Look! Can you see it? Can you see it? This is all for you."

GIFTS FROM ALSIVE

C.D. Gillikin

Utulu didn't know who to give the gifts to.

He had been told what the outside world was like, of course, but seeing it for himself was a different beast. He hadn't believed his eyes when his weeklong journey to the mainland finally paid off and he had first witnessed the city. Amidst the rocky maze of artifice, Utulu had made out that those moving shapes were all people—more people in five seconds than he had seen in his entire life. He had thought his family was big, but he had to revise that perception, tying his boat to a dock post next to vessels that could contain everyone he had ever known.

It was when he stepped onto the docks that he internalized the problem—he didn't know who to give the gifts to. Alsive hadn't prepared him for this. His family hadn't prepared him for this. In Utulu's nearly thirty years of life, he had never been without a purpose, without a guide, without his family and without Alsive.

But today he was alone, and he didn't know who to give the gifts to.

He stood amidst people bustling about the harbor—hauling fish, carrying boxes full of items Utulu did not understand, conversing. Conversing in his own language, he noticed, though their accent was strange to his ears. He figured his own might sound strange to them, in turn, but he knew at least that he could communicate.

The people here didn't look all that different to Utulu, really. He had been told fanciful stories of far-off travelers with hair of shining, flowing gold and skin so pale and thin one could see the blood underneath. The earth-brown skin, coiled black hair, and dark eyes of the strangers stood to remind him that though his home felt a world away, it had not been so far after all, in one sense.

He realized amid his reflections that one such stranger was looking at him, her eyes scrunched up and her mouth slightly open. Confused for a moment, it suddenly struck him what it must be that perplexed her—his red wooden mask, the symbol of his purpose and the face of Alsive. It was the only thing that would make him look any different from anyone else here. He weighed his options and headed over to speak with the strange woman. She seemed more nervous when he approached, but relaxed (if only a bit, he noticed) upon speaking with him. He said he had very important gifts that needed to be given, and she told him in return that if he were seeking someone to pay tribute to, his best bet would be to head up the coast and present what he had to the Iron King in his mountaintop fortress. Utulu didn't know how he felt about that, but he told her it was a splendid idea nonetheless, and after trading for some supplies, set off in his boat with nothing but a stranger's words to guide him.

It took Utulu several days' time to get to the place the stranger had mentioned, but he saw no mountains and no fortresses there. Upon finding a place to rest for the night, he was told by the bearded old innkeeper that he would have to spend another day rowing his boat up the river that divided this city in two, and then he would find the fortress looming above another city of stone and metal. The Innkeeper told Utulu two more things, as well: that he would have to climb all the way to the fortress up a thousand steps, and that he may be turned away by the King's many soldiers. But Utulu was not daunted—no, he *refused* to be daunted. He explained that this was his life's only goal, and that it did not matter how much time or effort it took, and in doing so, he convinced himself of it a little bit more. The next morning, he continued his journey, heading into the highlands and keeping his mind busy by singing.

When the tall blades of grass gave way to scrub and then that too began to yield to rocky hills, Utulu saw the city and the fortress that watched over it. As he found and made his way up the stairs, he felt his heart sink a little with each step toward his goal. He had found direction again—but he would lose it, soon, once he had completed his task. His legs shook more and more, and he found it harder to keep his balance. But as much as he did not know the future, he reminded himself that he had nowhere to return to anymore, and he made it to the top with ragged breath.

Utulu approached the high stone walls and came to a great iron gate carved with crocodile-headed warriors battling wild beasts. Soldiers clad in black and white brandished spears at Utulu and asked his purpose, but reluctantly opened the gate after he mentioned that he had come bearing gifts for the fortress's master. Another soldier led Utulu through sandy courtyards into a vast windowed room. The room was nearly bare save for tapestries embroidered with yet more scenes of violence, and a steep dais upon which rested an austere throne of gold, silver, jewels, and silks. Upon that throne sat the Iron King.

The King, like everyone else Utulu had met on this journey, stared at Utulu's mask for a moment. But Utulu had not expected that the King would smile at it. He stood up from his throne and descended the dais, his regalia of silk and steel covering his massive bulk. He told Utulu that while he had not been expecting a visit, it was more than welcome—if Utulu stated his purpose. Utulu eagerly replied to the King's command and explained that he was here to bring gifts to those who should rightfully have them. The King laughed and told Utulu to show him the gifts already.

Utulu took his heavy pack from his back—he was secretly relieved that it would be lighter after today—and reached into the bag. The King's authority reminded him of Alsive's, so he first procured the gift that reminded him the most of Alsive: a timepiece wrapped in a red cloth and counting the seconds on its own. The King watched Utulu with hungry eyes, and Utulu, not expecting such intensity, paused to look around the room. His eyes fell upon the tapestries again—he had been told stories, of course, and seen images of such brutality, but he had not known violence on a personal level. Alsive had never been slow to remind the family that any problems that could be solved without a fight should be, whether it had been children coming to blows over a stolen toy or elders at each other's throats over an insult. The King was like Alsive in that both could rule, but he did not surround himself with Alsive's teachings. Utulu put the gift back, and the King frowned.

Utulu's heartbeat quickened, and he lied to the King that he had a better gift for him in mind, trying to decide at the same time what that gift might be. Rummaging in his pack with trembling fingers, Utulu's hand grasped something solid, and he procured a hammer with the head spiked like the teeth of a monster. Utulu did not feel good about this gift, but he had stopped feeling good about the King too. He saw the potential for bloody brutality in both, and he presented the hammer to the King.

The King's eyes narrowed and Utulu felt like a small animal. But after a long pause, the King clasped his hand around the hammer's handle and took it from Utulu with a tense nod. Utulu stood and strapped his pack back on, and declined the King's offers to spend the night at the fortress. But when he headed down the stairs, Utulu got only halfway back to the city before sitting down and resting his head in his hands.

He still had twelve gifts to give out and no leads on who they might be for. When he thought of what might become of the King with the hammer, his mind raced. He sat, and he wallowed, but then he heard someone coming and looked up. A man clad in yellow was striding up the steps with purpose. Utulu wished he could share in this, and he looked at the man, who gave Utulu a wave in return and sat down beside him. Through their conversation, Utulu learned that the man had not come to petition the King for anything of political import, but simply felt that it would be good to come and see the fortress today. The yellow was also something he felt strongly about—he told Utulu it would bring him good fortune. Utulu considered the man odd. In all his life, Utulu had known only his family, whose purpose had been to serve Alsive and carry out its every edict. The only being Utulu had known that was guided entirely by its own design was Alsive itself.

Utulu reached into his bag to take the timepiece out once more, but he stopped himself. Alsive may have followed its feelings like this man, but it was not without reason. This man risked the wrath of the King and his soldiers by following his heart, and did not think to do anything to mitigate the danger. Alsive, meanwhile, was the wise overseer of Utulu's family, and everything it did it did not just with feeling, but with reason. So Utulu felt for a different gift—a compass, that he thought could serve as a guide to help the wandering soul—and gave it to him. As they parted ways, Utulu continued back to the city and got into his boat. He still had eleven gifts to give and only one lead: that his heart might guide him somewhere.

His feelings told him to go back to where he had first landed on the continent, and so he rowed toward the east once more. But his long and lonely journey was interrupted when he saw a second glow on the horizon during the sunset—this one on the land, to the south. He noticed a burning orange atop a hill and the far-off sounds of someone talking loudly near it. As he did not see anything else around and the landscape was especially serene, he figured the glow could only be one thing: a funeral pyre.

He had first intended to head further down the coast before stopping for the night out of respect for the mourners, but he realized something as he started to head away: there was only one voice he could hear. Only one soul telling the stories of the deceased to no one but the void and the sky. He thought that wasn't how it should be. He had thought that when he did the same two years before, telling of the fire in his mother's eyes and the times they sang together to nobody but their other dead kin as her body turned to ash like all the rest. He still wished he could go back in time to comfort himself on that day, but even Alsive had proclaimed that impossible when he had asked. So, he anchored his boat in the shallows and headed toward the fire to greet the lone mourner.

The old woman tending to the rites was taken aback when Utulu arrived, but seemed to him to be convinced of his harmlessness when he sat and listened to the stories she told about her husband. She wove them perfectly and he felt as if each and every one told him more about the the deceased—but her own life was absent. They spoke and slept and before they parted ways when the dawn came, Utulu continued to follow his heart and reached into his bag for a gift to give her. This time he did not reach for the timepiece—her wisdom, her age, her ability to look into the past were all like Alsive, but he more clearly saw where she differed from it as well: making herself smaller in her tales, taking up no space. So, he gave her a mirror, so that she might see herself anew and know how to tell her own story. As she headed back to her village, Utulu thought that his own story too was far from over, with ten gifts still remaining in his bag. But he also thought on what he might do when it was done, and wondered if even one person would stand by the pyre to mourn him when his time came.

With nothing but his whim and the hope that it would continue to bear fruit, he went back to the town he had landed in the first time. He had run out of food and had spent all of his money on supplies already, and logistical concerns were beginning to intrude on his holy mission. He wandered the dusty streets, not even knowing what to look for, when his eyes alighted on another man with a mask. A mask unlike his own, much more ornate and elaborate with multiple colors and a grin, but a mask nonetheless. Deciding once more to follow his heart, and in need of anyone to call a friend, Utulu went to talk with him.

The man turned out to be quite friendly by Utulu's reckoning, and so Utulu asked if he knew of any work that needed to be done in exchange for some food, drink, or coin. The man told him that he did in fact know where to find such a thing, because he needed passage to a small village a short way to the south by boat, and would be willing to pay some coin up front for the journey. Utulu accepted, and the two of them set out to this village, talking about the journeys they had undertaken recently. Utulu heard firsthand stories of far-off cities, thrilling adventures, and unusual people. But when pressed on why he needed to get to this village, the man's voice grew sad, and he refused to speak of it. Utulu, thinking he would do the same if asked about his past, decided not to press the issue.

While the two of them made camp on the shore partway to the village, Utulu felt he should give his benefactor a gift. Like Alsive, he had seen much and was able to tell many stories about his own life. But Alsive had only ever kept one secret from Utulu—that it was going to die—and it came clean about that after Utulu was the only one left on the island with it, so Utulu didn't think that counted. He gave the man a veil with which he could hide his face, and maybe, in some sense, hide his secrets. Keeping the pack strapped to him, Utulu fell asleep with a sense that he knew how to finish his mission, and still no sense of what he might do once his life's sole purpose had been attained.

Utulu awoke the next morning to find that the stranger and the boat were gone.

Utulu thought at first that it was some sort of prank or mistake, but after two hours of waiting had passed, he came to the conclusion that the man had stolen his boat. He cursed himself for being so gullible and wondered aloud if he had learned nothing from his childhood stories, if he had failed his mother, if he had failed Alsive. He reminded himself that even if he no longer had his boat, he still had the remaining nine gifts, and so he would have to carry on. Head heavy, he began to hike further south, hoping that at least the existence of the village was true.

To his relief, but not enough to lift his spirits from the pit they'd sunken into, he saw the village lights that evening and stumbled into town hungry. The villagers gawked at him and his mask, and told him that he would have to speak to their chief as they did not have an inn or any lodgings. He heard the fear in their voices and considered turning back—but he remembered, once again, that he had no home to return to, and so he went to speak with the chief.

The chief, it being evening, was with her family in their large stone brick home. Her four children stared at Utulu when he entered, but the chief dismissed them and told him to sit down for dinner by the fire. Her cooking was marvelous, and the chief and her husband asked for Utulu's story. He told them most of it, and he was not sure they believed him, but they offered him food and coin and a space on the floor to sleep on, if only he would clean and cook and mind the children in the daytime for as long as he stayed, as the chief would be busy guiding the village through a time when fish supplies were low and unease was high. Utulu was not sure if he wanted to do this, but he was not in a position to turn down their hospitality, and told them that he would love to.

For two weeks, Utulu watched the chief's children. Their personalities were all so different from one another, and Utulu wondered what it would have been like to have grown up in a big family. One child's strength was another's weakness—the perceptive eldest child was physically weak from childhood starvation, while her larger younger brother was reckless and tactless. Utulu wondered what his own weaknesses might be, and if his journey would have been any easier alongside others to bear it too, instead of him and his memories alone.

When the two weeks were up, Utulu had begun to feel much healthier, and he had heard of a ship that was set to pass by the village on its way further south. He hoped his coin would be enough to convince the captain to let him board and remain until they arrived at another city. He bid farewell to the chief and her family, but not before finding a gift to give her for all of her aid. Her ruling power made her like Alsive, and the Iron King too, but her gentle hand in guiding her children and her village through even hard times made him understand that she had a unique talent for making the best of the bad. And so, he gave her a filter to purify the things around her, before he hailed the boat and swam on board with eight gifts in his pack.

Utulu found that things continued to look up for him as the captain, initially bewildered and frightened by a masked man swimming to his ship and requesting to stay, reluctantly allowed him to come along to the next port in exchange for some of the coin. Utulu found himself sharing a cabin with a man surrounded by many bags and cases. Upon asking about them, Utulu learned that the man was an artist and a musician, and he was heading back from foreign lands with instruments and pigments he could not buy at home. The man and his songs kept Utulu company over the days at sea, and as the man sang of far-off places and historical heroes, Utulu thought that he might like to learn more about them once he had given away the gifts.

The man's boundless imagination made him deserving of one such gift, the way Utulu saw it—Alsive, in the last few years when it had just been the two of them on the island, had been fond of telling stories about what the world might be like in the years after its death. One of the gifts Utulu still had was a brush with fine bristles well-suited to painting, and he gave this to the artist before they parted ways on the docks in yet another new city, with only seven gifts in Utulu's pack now.

Utulu quickly learned that this city was not under the rule of the Iron King, a fact which lightened Utulu's shoulders more than taking his pack off. Deciding to save the rest of his coin for food, Utulu spent his first night in this city on the street, where he found a young man dressed in rags. Utulu went to ask the boy his story, but he was not very forthcoming. Utulu did not trust this initially, but when a group of people came to demand Utulu's few coins at the point of a knife, it was the ragged boy who came to distract them and allowed Utulu to escape. Utulu asked him why he would help, and he simply responded that he knew what it was like to be kicked while already down. As Alsive too had known struggle and misery in the final months of its centuries-long lifespan, Utulu gave the boy a gift: a cage of sorts that he hoped would serve to protect and strengthen the boy and allow him to stand up not just for others, but himself as well. As Utulu headed away, his next job taking him to another city further south, he wondered what his own life might have been like if he had stood on his own as opposed to standing for his family and for Alsive. He figured that with just six gifts of the original thirteen in his pack and his journey having taken only a month thus far, he might have time to find out.

His employer, a lone merchant unaffiliated with guilds and conglomerates, turned out to make good conversation. Beneath her wide-brimmed hat covered in jingling handmade charms as they walked through the savanna, she and Utulu told stories to each other, a ritual that he found familiar by now. She told him of her life as a child, a slave, an artisan, a mercenary, and now a merchant. The curious thing, she said, was that she had never thought she'd grow up to be any of those things, and in her childhood she had expected that she would grow up to be a farmer.

Alsive had been many things over its life. It had told Utulu of its time revered by the people of the mainland as the mightiest of their gods, and then of its time abandoned on the island with nobody but the Faithful and finally the family to keep it company. Even though it had already been old, Alsive's personality still changed a little in the years Utulu had known it, growing more decisive and then more reflective when it was just Alsive and Utulu left. Once they got to the gates of their destination, Utulu gave his employer a gift too—a set of bellows that he hoped might breathe even more life into her already vibrant existence. She seemed confused, but Utulu could tell from the way she handled the instrument that it belonged in her hands. Now alone once more in another fortified city, Utulu had merely five gifts remaining.

Utulu found that he craved stories now, the same way he craved certain foods, and so he headed to the library in this town, a dusty old place, which he found rather meager, but it would have to suffice for now. Spending his money on street food and his days on reading, he came to notice another patron who came to the library every day. Clad in rags, the young woman was tiny and frail-looking, but her eyes were hard and sharp. Utulu did not wish to disturb her, in part because he thought she might take offense to being disturbed at all, but he was impressed by her dedicated studies of myth, history, art, and medicine in whatever texts she could glean from the paltry shelves.

One day, Utulu overheard some of the staff talking about another library, a much larger one, in a much larger city a week's walk up the wide river. Satisfied that he had exhausted the stories here, and tiring of eating fish every day, he resolved to head that way to see what he could find. But before he departed, he silently left a gift for the young woman—she did not fit the timepiece either, as Alsive had always been a welcoming presence, but her knowledge and curiosity were worthy of a lens so that she might see even more. Not wishing to intrude by asking her thoughts on it, Utulu simply headed onwards to his next destination, four gifts now left in his pack.

The road to the river's jewel was a straightforward one, but the city's roads themselves wound upon one another, and Utulu became lost on his way to the library. With the sun quickly sinking and an empty stomach and aching feet, Utulu headed into a public house he found in his wandering, and used the last of his coin on food, drink, and a room for a week—the rates were out of his price range, but the innkeeper insisted that what he had would be fine.

To his delight, Utulu did not have to go as far as the library to glean more stories. After his second day at the inn, a mercenary returned from his mission. He was an older man, for a warrior, with a scarred face and a wooden leg, and he was all too happy to tell of this mission and missions past. Utulu still spent his days at the library, but he spent his nights drinking and relaxing as he and the innkeeper listened to the old man tell his tales.

From the chatter in the inn, Utulu heard that there would be a festival to celebrate the fall equinox in a town in the highlands a little ways north of this city. He used to do the same on the island with his family, all at

Alsive's behest. He knew that the people here did not revere Alsive and had not since before he was born, but he wondered if this was some fragment of Alsive's mark upon the world from when all knew it reigned supreme. Sad to bid his new companions farewell, and a little surprised to realize he might have called them his friends, he left a gift for them both. To the old man he gave a knife—though Utulu had not grown more comfortable with violence since he had met the King, he could tell that the man was angry with the injustice in the world, and wished to use bloodshed not as its own end or as a tool for power, but as a tool to make things right. To the innkeeper who had been so giving, he gave a box in which she could find more treasures, trusting her to know how to give them out as he had given the gifts himself. With three and then two gifts remaining, Utulu began his walk to the highlands.

During this leg of his journey, Utulu reflected upon where he had come from, and where he would go upon giving out the last gifts. The timepiece—the gift most like Alsive—was one of the two he still had. He was not sure if there was truly more importance to that gift above all the rest, but he could not banish that notion from his head. He found the fact that any one gift might be more like Alsive than the others very strange. The gifts had been all he found in Alsive's place when it had breathed its last and faded from the world. They were all that remained of it, so why would this one, uniquely, keep time just like Alsive had?

He thought again of the values he found embodied in the people he had given gifts to so far. Each and every one of them had reminded him of Alsive in some way or another. But as he thought more, the picture grew muddier. Was he ascribing these traits to those people because he had not wanted Alsive to go? Did he ascribe value to the timepiece in order to hold on to something that had been Alsive, refusing to let his reason to live go? He did not have answers or the time to come up with them before he came to the town he had heard about and the equinox arrived.

What first struck him was how this festival was unlike the ones he had celebrated on his island. There were more people, of course, but there was also drinking, trade, and games. But even within these, Utulu saw singing, dancing, and prayer—all of the things he had done on this day each year for Alsive. The heat of the sun proving intolerable under his mask for too long, Utulu took shade underneath the awning of an unused market stall, sitting behind its crude wooden counter and looking out at the festival behind Alsive's eyes.

He almost didn't notice when a young woman with long braids approached him, but he turned back to see her at the right time, clearly startling her. He recognized her from one of the other stalls earlier, selling grains and fruits presumably grown on her farm. She asked about his purpose here, and as he had not yet finished and been released from his sacred duty, he told her that he was here to give gifts. She bit her lip and clasped her hands as they conversed, and Utulu knew these gestures all too well—he did the same when something was bothering him. So he asked that she speak her mind, and to his surprise, she laid her worries plain. A nostalgia for her family and the way she had always lived here, but an uncertainty about where to go next in her life. A terror that she might never see what the world had to offer, and might live her whole life in one place, doing one simple thing forever. She sighed heavily at the end of her story, as if she regretted reopening her own wounds.

But her story got Utulu thinking. He thought about the gifts again and why and when he had given them. He thought about how he had given them to people who would be able to use them. And he thought that this young woman could use a reminder that she had not run out of time. His heart beating quickly at the thought of losing his friend a second time, he nevertheless knew his journey would have to continue, and he gave the young woman the timepiece. Then, Utulu had but one gift left to give.

Utulu sat underneath a tree outside of town after the festival ended. Sitting by a small fire and removing his mask, he drew the final gift from his bag. He had overlooked this one thus far—a staff, or a walking stick perhaps, that appeared to be made from bone. Something that would anchor its holder to the ground below, and would aid them in a long journey to come, no matter what that may be. Its knobbed head fit his palm perfectly, and he stood to lean upon it. One last piece of Alsive was at his side to guide him—no, he thought, to help him guide himself.

And so, when morning came, with all of the gifts given, Utulu took his staff in hand and set off to find his next journey.

RETAIL

Kaleb A. Brown

It was a dark and stormy night; the rain fell in seething, biblical torrents—except at occasional intervals, when it was checked by a violent gust of wind that swept up the streets (in San Jose, where our scene lies), rattling along the housetops, strangling the trees, and fiercely agitating the golden shine of the streetlights, rendering it a blurry, diffuse yellow.

Not that the patrons of Sunshine Value Kingdom could particularly tell. During the brief breaks from eighties rock over the speakers, they might hear the slapping of rain on the old roof, rhythmically popping like a snare drum, vying for supremacy over the radio host's enthusiasm. But other than that, they were blissfully ignorant of the chaos that lay beyond the sliding double doors.

A good deal of Sunshine's workers, however, had almost aggravatingly exceptional hearing, so they were quite aware of the rain's assault on San Jose that October eve. They were keenly aware of the rock as well. Every guitar twang, every heartfelt, anguished Bon Jovi belt practically vibrated through most of the workers. They begged their boss to change the music, at least every once in a while, but he was adamant that the channel would never change. The customers were used to it, the boss argued; it kept them comfortable. And the customers' comfort came first. Then the boss's. Then the workers'.

Daciana, currently manning cash register number two, was a fan of classic rock and even she had grown weary of "Summer of '69" after hearing it for what felt like the fiftieth time that day. The shredding metal and electronic beeps of the scanner were all now monotonous noise to her, an unwanted, yet effective lullaby. Her head nodded before jerking back up to attention. The last thing she needed was her boss giving her an earful. She half thought she might just snap next time he got lippy with her. Just split him open and drink the blood with one of the straws in aisle three. Wouldn't that be nice?

She stifled a yawn as she continued to scan. But wouldn't a teenie weenie nap be just great? These days, her eyes had more bags than—shit she'd have to bag these. Where the hell was Lupus? Oh right, it was a full moon. In a perfect world, he'd have been given the day off.

Ponnie, a cash register over, was having her own battle with fatigue.

Cereal.

Beep

Ramen.

Beep

Milk.

Beep

Eggs.

Beep

Fresh produce.

Goddammit, let's see, what is this, she thought. *An orange? It's a big-ass orange, but whatever.* She punched in the six-digit code and began to hand the fruit over to Tom, one of the baggers. Then she paused and scrunched up her face. "Oh fuck me, this is a grapefruit, not an orange. Who the hell likes grapefruit, anyway?" She gave a defeated sigh. "Shit, hold on, I have to redo this."

Tom scrunched his eyebrows in concern. "Ponnie, language," he quietly chastised.

Ponnie simply rolled her eyes and tugged her ponytail the way she did whenever she was agitated. "Oh, piss off." Fucking boy scout. She sighed. No, that wasn't fair. It's not his fault.

Karina, pushing a shopping cart to the front of the store, stopped when she was between Ponnie and Daciana, a great smile on her face. It was a comical sight, a woman not an inch over four feet, wearing a tall, pointed red hat, pushing a shopping cart as fast as she could manage. She looked like she could either be twelve or sixty. She turned toward Ponnie, holding up her index finger.

"Turn those frowns upside down," Karina exclaimed in an accent that Ponnie couldn't quite place, but Daciana recognized as Scandinavian. "Only one more hour until closing!"

Ponnie gave a half-smile to appease her chipper coworker. Karina used to irritate Ponnie to no end when she first began working at Sunshine; everyone had the same initial experience with her. Being around Karina, always the Pollyanna, was akin to seeing someone's glee over eating ice cream while you have to grin and bear being stoned. It wasn't that Karina had a better experience working at Sunshine; it was just that she thought she could boost morale if she filled the drab white walls of the place with a golden cheer. Everyone eventually came around to her. It was very difficult to stay mad at someone who spent what meager pay she had buying gifts for coworkers.

"One more hour," Daciana repeated. The last of fifteen. And from experience, she knew this would be the longest, counting the clock by the minutes, the seconds, anticipating the moment when she'd finally be granted release from her retail prison.

***

The speakers chirped with a glorious tone and a message of salvation, recorded by Karina.

"Attention shoppers, it is ten o'clock p.m., Sunshine Value Land is closed. Please proceed to checkout for any final purchases. I repeat, it is ten o'clock p.m."

It was Daciana's turn to start the ritual. "No sight of any customers in register two," she called out. Tom shifted awkwardly, feeling like he was left out of some sort of inside joke.

"None at three," called Ponnie gleefully.

"None at four," said a worker at the fourth cash register.

"None at five!"

"Or six!"

"Not seven!"

"Or eight!"

"Nein here!"

"Check on back, my aisle men," Daciana called with a smile, getting swept up in the energy of her fellow wage slaves.

"And women," cried out Lizzi. "None in aisles ten to six."

"And none," began Declan, in his melodic Irish accent. Daciana stifled a laugh at the sound of his feet pitter-pattering to scan the aisle. "In aisles five to one."

"And drumroll please," said Daciana. The entire store filled with the rumbling sound of the employees furiously banging on their legs, the walls, the shelves, anything they could get their overworked hands on.

Knowing the ritual, Karina dramatically stepped into the store after the automatic doors permitted her entrance. She was soaked from the rain, but she didn't let that wash away her smile. Hands on her hips and head raised high, she called out, loud enough that her high-pitched voice echoed throughout the store. "And with all the carriages having left the kingdom—"

"We're allowed to leave the land," cried Daciana. The store broke into rapturous applause. Daciana could practically taste it—a nice, small, cold place to sleep.

"Freedom!" Snefuru cheered from cash register six.

"Home," called another employee.

"You can come on out, Lupus," laughed Ponnie.

They all went quiet as a torturous howl pierced the air. The door of the break room slammed open and they heard the sound of a wild animal bound through the store, gnarled, long claws scraping the squeaky-clean tiles of the floor. Once he reached the front of the store, Lupus rose and gave another howl. His yellow uniform was bursting at the seams from his gained mass. Tufts of fur seeped from between his buttons. His now canine face was framed by overgrown hair. "Sunshine's closed so now it's time to act like an animal," he growled, garnering laughs from his coworkers.

Their smiles quickly melted as they jerked their heads at the sound of their boss's air horn that he blew whenever he demanded their attention.

His rolls bouncing as he stepped, Mr. Harold Sunshine himself slowly walked down the front of the store. He looked around with a smug smile, knowing that no matter what performances his employees put on, he was the ruler of this kingdom. Like his father before him and like his son would be after him.

He held up his hand. "Hold your horses, people." He glanced at Ponnie, earning him an ill-concealed sneer.

He stopped in his tracks, looking up as if he was searching for something in the rafters. He turned on the ball of his feet and pointed at Tom. "You, son. You may go for the day."

Tom gave a little bow. "Thank you, sir," he said before walking off.

Ponnie shook her head. It wasn't his fault. She was sure he felt bad, too, how separate he was from the rest of them. While he was friendly enough, he'd never be able to connect with his fellow employees. No one ever brought it up with him, in part due to how obvious it was. He was from a different world. He was treated better. He'd never feel the way they felt, even if he could empathize.

Mr. Sunshine waited for Tom to leave before continuing to speak. "The rest of you, you have to work overtime." He closed his eyes, knowing beforehand that the collective groan was coming. "No moaning and groaning. Tomorrow's the first day of November and you know what that means—Thanksgiving, and more importantly, Black Friday. This place needs to be primed and ready to be a selling machine. I want this place stocked; I want it clean and I want it—"

"That's a load of crap. You can't keep us overtime when most of us have been here for fifteen hours," Daciana said.

Mr. Sunshine gave a chuckle. "Can't I? What are you going to do? Quit? Tell someone?"

"Will there at least be pay?" asked Karina.

Mr. Sunshine laughed loudly. "Well that's a stupid question, isn't it?"

Ponnie gave an angry donkey kick to the door of the cash register area.

"You break it, you buy it," Mr. Sunshine snapped.

"I was just stretching my legs, sir," she said with a frown.

"Oh, good. Well in that case, take stock of the aisles, see what we need more of," Mr. Sunshine chuckled.

Ponnie mumbled something under her breath before opening the door to the cash register area and awkwardly maneuvering out. She galloped down aisle two, her four equine legs working their sinewy muscles as the aisle filled with the sound of her clops.

Mr. Sunshine turned to Karina, trying her best to maintain her smile, the sides of her lips quivering. "You, mop up the puddle at the door."

"But Mr. Sunshine, you know the mop's too tall for—"

"Did I ask for your complaints?" Karina was silent as she looked toward the ground. "That's right. Now wipe that shit up before I fire your ass." Karina slowly moved toward the supply closet, sniffling. "Ándale," cried Mr. Sunshine.

Daciana looked intensely at Mr. Sunshine's neck. Say she did bite him. What would his blood taste like? She was always unsure if blood tasted like what was in your stomach or heart.

He turned to her. "You, go clean the rafters. Dust them off and make sure there aren't any birds or anything up there."

Daciana sighed. "Aye, aye, captain." In a flash, she was enveloped in a column of black smoke. Where she stood, a camp of screeching bats flew upwards.

***

As the dismal night dragged on, painstaking minute by painstaking minute, the sour atmosphere was almost palpable. Hardly anyone was in the mood for chatting. Even if they did, Mr. Sunshine patrolling the store like a guard dog quickly shut them up. However, as he went to the lavatory to take care of business, the employees were given brief respite. The eighties rock continued to play over the speakers, however. *St. Elmo's Fire* served as a grim reminder: Even when it was overcast, the sun was still present.

Snerferu, covered from head to toe in linen cloth, once a mighty pharaoh, was now being paid less than his laborers. He did his best to make himself scarce, knowing that if Mr. Sunshine ran out of toilet paper, he'd demand some of the dead man's wrapping.

Blaine, the horseman with a jack-o-lantern in place of his lost head, was called into the store. Due to his appearance, he was usually out at the front of the parking lot, twirling signs. Currently, he was helping Ponnie carry the new shipments to storage. Ponnie laughed at Blaine's flirtatious jokes. She was the only one who understood him. The other employees just couldn't figure out how to understand the words of one without a head.

Daciana, in the toy section, looked over her shoulder to make sure Mr. Sunshine hadn't left the restroom. Finding the coast clear, she quickly opened one of the doll packages and stuffed the blond figure in her pocket. She then gingerly placed a similarly sized winged blond boy in the package. A sleep-deprived pixie was one of the saddest things you could see.

"Sleep tight, I'll come back for you in a bit, Angus," she said before moving the box to the back.

"Tampering with my product? I should have you thrown out," growled a voice from behind.

If she had a heart, Daciana imagined it would be furiously beating out her chest at times like these. She quickly turned around before blowing a breath. It was just Declan, now giggling like a child.

Daciana furrowed her brow. "I could punt you for that."

"Aye, but you wouldn't, now. You're much too nice."

Daciana sighed, folding her arms. "More like stupid. Nice doesn't mean having to put up with that beast of a man."

Susan "Spectra" Daniels, blue and softly glowing, floated through the shelving. She had actually worked at the store in life. After dying due to negligence, she continued working for Mr. Sunshine. Some said she haunted the place. She just needed the cash.

Daciana and Declan nearly jumped when she began wailing. As it turned out, this was just her normal speaking voice. "More like desperate. If we all could quit, I'm sure we would."

Declan quickly spoke, in part to stop Spectra from talking. "I certainly would, but we're stuck here."

Daciana slumped against a shelf and closed her eyes. "Yeah, there's nothing we can do about it." A sad silence fell over the trio.

Play the game, you know you can't quit until it's won
Soldier on, only you can do what must be done
You know, in some ways you're a lot like me
You're just a prisoner, and you're tryin' to break free
I can see a new horizon underneath the blazing sky.

Daciana opened her eyes and straightened.

"Ugh, I know, it's awful," Declan said, shaking his head.

"This song was new when I was alive," said Spectra.

"No, no. Look, for better or for worse, we're stuck here, but that doesn't mean we just have to take it. We don't have to accept this prison."

"Oh Lord, John Parr's got to her." Declan shook his head. "Even the best ones fall eventually."

"Oh, come on. There's one of him and so many of us," exclaimed Daciana.

"Well that's true, but he still got in your head," said Declan.

Daciana scrunched up her face. "Huh? No, not John Parr. Sunshine."

"Oh. Well, with his money and legal standing, I'm sure it evens out," Declan said.

"Then it's a fair fight!" Daciana sped out of the aisle. "Employees! Urgent meeting in the break room!" Spectra and Declan could do naught but look at each other nervously before making their way to the break room.

***

The large break room was filled almost to capacity with the employees as they shifted uncomfortably. Half their attention was devoted to watching Daciana at the front of the room and the other half was devoted to nervously whipping their heads toward the door, expecting Mr. Sunshine to burst in.

"Look, Mr. Sunshine's going to be off the john any second now," Daciana began.

Tony, a lich whose hood covered a skeletal head, spoke. "Yes, so let's get back to our posts," he said quickly, voice full of terror.

Frank von Stein raised his shambling, bluish arm. "Can I get my other arm right quick? It fell off on the way here."

"Everyone, focus. No, we're not leaving, Tony. And we can get your arm after we're through, Frankie. Aren't you all sick and tired of being pushed around? Do you know California's minimum wage?"

Karina raised her hand. After Daciana pointed to her, she answered. "Twelve dollars."

Daciana nodded. "That's right, twelve dollars. We get $3.75 an hour and we're not even paid for overtime, which we shouldn't even be forced to do. We need to demand more for ourselves."

Ponnie scoffed. "That's easy for you to say, Ms.-I'm-practically-a-person. You can walk out of here, apply to McDonald's, and none will be the wiser of what you are." Blaine seemed to make an affirmative something. Noise? Gesture? Feeling? It was hard to say.

Daciana recoiled as if slapped. She was always aware of how, unlike some of her colleagues, her identity wasn't externally apparent. "See, that's part of the problem. We are people, even if we're not treated like it."

Ponnie gave a you-know-what-I-meant scoff.

"I know I might not have it as hard as some of you, but believe me, if Sunshine didn't keep a stash of blood pouches in the break room, I probably *would* bite someone, and that would get me in more hot water than if someone saw horse legs."

Ponnie was about to argue when Karina raised her hands high in appeasement. "I think what Daciana is trying to say is that even if it might not seem like it sometimes, we're in the same boat. From Tony," she said, nodding at the lich, "to Lizzie," a mostly humanoid, but fairly scaly half-dragon that proved what happens in Vegas doesn't always stay in Vegas, "to Declan," who *should* have no need for this job as per his inherited pot of gold, but his brother had apparently stolen it.

"So what I'm suggesting is we band together to get our dues."

Everyone turned to the door as it burst open. Through it stepped a very red-faced Mr. Sunshine. His face drained of its crimson color once he processed what he was seeing: his employees, in one spot, apparently staring him down.

Daciana couldn't help but smile. He was quivering.

"What the hell is this?" Mr. Sunshine asked.

Ponnie smiled. "This," she began throwing her hands out, "is apparently our little revolution." Even though she had disagreed with Daciana, she always got a kick out of getting a rise out of her boss.

Declan spoke up. "Give us fair wages. Give us fair hours. Or else."

"Or else what?" Mr. Sunshine folded his arms.

"Or else we sue. Then find somewhere else to work," Karina said, darkly. Daciana and other employees tried their best not to gawk. She didn't plan that far. She wanted justice of some sort, but suing?

Mr. Sunshine held his gaze with Karina before his lips curled upward. He began to giggle. The giggles gave way to chuckles. The chuckles transformed into laughter. Then he started to heartily howl, clutching his stomach, eyes closed tightly. He pounded a fist on his leg. He opened his eyes to see that none of his employees were laughing.

His laughter died down before he raised his eyebrows. "Oh, you're serious." He began to chuckle once more. "Do you really think getting the law involved is the best move? You're not even supposed to be working here. If the pigs catch wind of you, I'm sure the spook show will scoop you up before you know what hit you. How does that sound? Being locked up in Area 51 and experimented on because you thought you could sue me."

"We're still people, we have rights," wailed Spectra.

"Turn on a TV sometime. Tell me if the people on commercials are freaks like you," said Mr. Sunshine.

"One, don't call us 'freaks.' Two, we can't *afford* television," said Frank.

"I don't see why you're all getting uppity. You need me a hell of a lot more than I need you. No one else would hire you monsters, they'll just call the cops. I'm the only one who will give you what you need to function in the work day. Where would Ms. Dracula be without her blood pouches? Dragon Chick without her lizard food?"

"We'd be grateful if you didn't treat us like shit, didn't call us 'monsters.' We're 'uppity' because we're decent people, more than you'll ever be," said Lupus.

"You *need* me. You can't feed your pups without me."

Hearing a hint of pleading in his voice, Daciana tried one last time. "Last call. Give us what you owe us or we'll take it."

"I don't want to see your asses in my store ever again."

Daciana smiled. "Then we'll see *you* in court," she said with a cheeky smile. She led the rest of the employees out of the break room. They ripped off their name tags and threw them on the ground as they left the kingdom.

SEIZURE

Kaleb A. Brown

The hunting knife Nashala had been gifted before her Seizing hadn't proved good for anything save chopping off her forest of voluminous, onyx hair. She tightly grabbed a fistful of hair, holding it taut before flashing the metal, and the curls plummeted to the dirt she knelt in. She didn't look at the hair as it fell. Seeing the hair she was so used to lying dead on the ground might make her hesitate.

Her massive hair had been a symbol of unchallenged beauty and status in the city-state of Lunn, but the raw, wild jungle cared not about human measures of fitness. In Shana, the spirit land, the only metric of success was if you could survive. In Shana, the hair she had taken so much pride in had only hindered her. Her hair made Nashala so hot that the headband she wore became slick with sweat. It felt as if she had dived into a river. Her hair repeatedly got snagged by low-hanging branches. Most alarming to her, insects took a keen liking to the mobile shelter. After the third worm she took out of her hair, she felt she was better without it. Besides, it would grow back.

She was surprised how easy it was—destroying what she had cultivated for the past twenty years. After the first tuft of hair fell, the next ones came easier and easier until she touched scalp. She took a glance down and saw the black bush of hair below.

Now that her hair was getting sparse, she was starting to second-guess her decision. Her hair had always been a part of her, always helped to shape her perception of self: brown eyes, caramel skin, toned physique, and a beautiful black halo of hair. She hesitated a moment before quickly cutting out some of her last strands and yanking out others by hand, leaving only a wispy, thin layer. She looked at her reflection in a nearby pond, quickly turning away from the strange, near-bald woman who looked back. She didn't let her alien appearance bother her, however. After all, abandoning old notions of self was exactly what the Seizing was all about.

All teenagers in Lunn dreamed of the Seizing. It was not mandatory to take the trial upon becoming an adult, but the tales elders spun about normal people taking on the traits of great beasts were so fantastical, so gripping, so inspiring that few Lunnites passed up the opportunity to thrust themselves into the spirit lands in hopes of becoming something greater.

The Seizing, as the name suggested, involved forcibly acquiring something from another. A successful Seizing demanded the theft of a soul. On their twentieth birthday, Lunnites had the option to be released to the southern peninsula, where Shana lay. Shana teemed with fauna and it was said that in the forest, souls easily left their fleshy prisons. This made the forest the perfect place to snatch the soul of another. Using a weapon coated or tipped with Spiritrock, a Lunnite undergoing seizing would wound an animal, causing its soul to enter them. The process would imbue them with traits of the slain animal. Many stories told of the undesirable traits of a person fading, being replaced with the honorable qualities of the acquired soul. Those with a wolf soul would become great team players, those with raven souls were smart, baboon souls were good-spirited, and so on. Some stories, however, painted a grim tale: one where the person was irrevocably changed. Their bodies were hijacked by a terribly powerful soul. Their beings rotted out of their very body, every aspect of themselves lost to the unforgiving jungle of Shana. The eager Lunnites would find they were the ones who had their souls stolen by the animals, and not vice-versa.

Nashala always shuddered when she heard stories like that. She was quite fond of herself and couldn't imagine her soul being shoved out of her beautiful body, forced to drift into the wind of Shana, pitifully wailing to anyone who could hear.

Nashala's double-bladed sword, shaped like the letter Y, rested in its hard, ivory sheath on her bare thigh save for her shorts. She walked through the jungle, shoving low-hanging branches out of her way and quickly slapping insects that landed on her skin before they could even think of biting her. Despite the noise she was making, she was able to hear stumbling through the forest. She had trained for this day for many years; she doubted there was anything that could catch her unawares in Shana, even as brutal as it was said to be. She stopped in her tracks and closed her eyes, listening intently.

Heavy breathing and pained, half-aborted snorts. She scrunched up her face. Some mammal. Four-legged? No, two-legged? Both. Well, however many legs it walked on, given how much noise it made as it walked, it was quite large.

After a moment of listening, Nashala decided she had been idle long enough: it was time for some action. She cautiously began walking forward and heard sniffing before the nearby creature broke into a run. She matched it, bolting forward, pumping her arms as the bramble scratched her thighs and shins. She saw a part in the greenery and quickly turned her head to see that the creature was dark and, as she expected, quite large.

She burst into a clearing and spun around on her booted heel to face a snarling, velvet bear bounding toward her. Even as it ran, she could see the sickening white froth that spilled out of its barred fangs along with its wide, bloodshot eyes. Rabies.

Fearlessly, Nashala ducked as the bear leapt up and swiped at her head. As she pressed herself low to the ground, she gave a powerful kick to the bear's abdomen, causing it to tumble. She quickly got to her feet and unsheathed her hunting sword. The bear had but a moment to rise before it found its head brutally bashed by the blunt arm of the Y. A split second later, Nashala had flipped the blade and severed the bear's head with the sharp arm. She turned around, wiped the blood on the grass, sheathed her sword, and continued walking, not even considering the corpse of the bear for Seizing.

It wasn't that Nashala found the bear a disagreeable candidate for her Seizing because of its rabidness; souls were immune to the diseases of the flesh and mind. Bears weren't considered small-fry for a Seizing, either. They were quite respectable souls. Many a great warrior, businessman, and artist touted having bear souls, with the tattoo to match. But Nashala had her eyes on a soul much grander. She didn't wish to simply be respected; she wished to be revered. Nashala had her eyes set on the soul of a lion, King of the Jungle. With a lion's soul, she was sure she'd be recognized as the undisputed Chief of Lunn.

She walked through the forest. Her boots made wet prints in the mud and the cool spring breeze tickled her bare shoulders. Nashala took in all the sounds around her. From her studies, she was certain of which sounds belonged to which animal—the scuttle of duikers on the grass and the whooping and hollering of monkeys. None of the sounds she heard belonged to her prize.

Nashala heard barking and stopped in her tracks with a sigh. She folded her arms as a large troop of baboons emerged from the trees and dropped to the ground below to cross her path. She paid no heed to the magnificent golden fur of the animals, nor their long tails or their long faces that resembled a dog's. Even when she couldn't proceed, Nashala's mind was only focused on finding a lion.

The last of the baboons began to cross: a mother and her child. They stopped to look at Nashala before bounding off upon seeing the young woman stomping and hissing at the pair.

Nashala continued her hunt. She tried to resist thinking about the child gibbon following its parent's lead. She needed her mind, her sharpest tool, clear of distractions, but it was no use.

She remembered a caring hand brushing the hair from her eyes. The hair that was no longer there. She felt its owner's warmth loom over her before a kiss was planted on Nashala's forehead.

"When I grow up, I want to be just like you," Nashala remembered saying in a voice that was much younger.

The woman at the side of her bed smiled. She looked a lot like Nashala. "I certainly hope you don't grow up to be me. You're free to be whoever you like. When you grow up, you'll want to be your own person."

The mother baboon reminded Nashala a bit of her own mother. Nashala tried not to think of her. It was too distracting.

Her family, her father and grandparents, were the ones who convinced her that she should shoot for nothing less than a lion when she was old enough to partake in the Seizing. They told her that she must become the next chief. It was suggested Nashala quit weight training and start training rigorously for the Seizing. If not for her family, she would have been satisfied with the soul of the bear that she had felled.

Nashala did not resent her family. She loved them quite dearly, loved them enough to discard her desires for theirs. She wanted to make them happy, especially after they had been so disappointed.

For Nashala's grandparents, their family as the leader of Lunn was a memory. For her father, it was a dream unfulfilled. For her late mother, it had been a dream unwanted.

Nashala's grandmother had ruled Lunn for nearly forty years, leading the city-state to prosperity. As per succession mandate, her daughter, Nashala's mother, was next in line to rule. Nashala's father had married her mother in part thanks to the pretense that he'd be the chief's husband.

But that wasn't the case.

In a decision that made her family's jaws drop permanently to the floor, Nashala's mother declined the position of chief. A suitable replacement was found in a matter of days. Her family's dream was gone in a snap. Nashala's mother stated that she wanted to be a caring mother and an excellent baker more than she wanted the pressure of ruling an entire city-state. Her family didn't care about the reasons; they cared that she had thrown away not only her future, but theirs as well.

Nasahala was born soon after. Despite adamantly pursuing what her mother discarded, Nashala was close to her mother and never questioned her decision. It was hard loving and respecting her mother, as well as her father and grandparents, despite their conflicting viewpoints on such a crucial matter, but Nashala did her best to favor neither side's opinion over the other, and her parents did their best not to argue around her.

Nashala's mother died when she was eleven. Whether her family's tears were fake or real, she couldn't say. Regardless, it didn't take long for them to dry. Her family began grooming her. They'd give condolences while making it clear that her mother had chosen the wrong path in life. They told Nashala that it was her duty, as the daughter, to do what her mother couldn't. It was her duty to make the family great once more.

Even if her family wasn't in power, they were well-off. She wanted to live her life as a stylish noble and socialite. Maybe she'd serve in the army, too, or maybe just as a hunter: anything to keep her active during the day after socializing at night. But her parents quickly put her adolescent dreams to rest. Unlike her mother, there would be no ifs, ands, or buts. They assured Nashala that she was going to be the next chief. She didn't argue. Without Nashala's mother there to defend herself, Nashala's family convinced her that her mother had been short-sighted, selfish, and hedonistic.

Two of Lunn's adages were "The mind of the elder has soaked more knowledge than the mind of the brat" and "The young baboon who rebels against its parents soon starves from ignorance." The parent knew best. Besides, Nashala wanted her family to be happy.

Nashala delved deeper and deeper into Shana, closer and closer to the lion, her family's ticket back to greatness. She hoisted herself over boulders, picked her way through branches, waded through streams, and fought with beasts for the better part of a day. She was bound to be close. Nashala was near the center of Shana in a little under two days. She would have been there sooner if she hadn't rested the previous day. It would take the average Lunnite the better part of four days to cover the ground she did. But she wasn't like the average Lunnite. For weeks, months, and years, these days played out in her head. Most simply lived their lives until they became of age. But not Nashala. She couldn't mess this up. Not after the family that cared for her after all those years imbued her with their hopes and dreams. She was ready.

So why was she so wet with sweat that it looked like she had just gone for a swim? Why were her hands shaking so badly that the only way to stop them was by gripping her thighs so tight that she had marks where her fingernails touched skin?

Now wasn't the time to get cold feet. She could take down a lion, she had trained for this. She swallowed and broke into a jog.

Soon, Nashala found herself nearing a rocky clearing. She stopped moving and tried to quiet her breathing as she crept to a part in the branches. She peered through the opening and saw a smooth, long rock. It took every bit of restraint she had not to gasp at what she saw next. Lean muscles, the gait full of confidence, the long tail with a tuft at the end, the golden mane. There it was, exactly as she dreamed it would be. Her lion. Her soul.

She swallowed. She'd show no fear or hesitation. She got low to the ground as she began to emerge from trees. The lion didn't seem to notice her, occupied with something else. She turned her head, curious. What could be so important? She saw two gray calves backing away from the lion who gave threatening, guttural growls. It wasn't very honorable, but with the lion distracted, she'd be able to ambush it.

She began to sneak toward the lion, sword ready. She raised it over her head when an explosion of sound burst behind her, nearly causing her to drop the weapon. It was so loud it threatened to split her ears and head both. The sound was like someone blowing on a horn with all their might followed by a throaty, inhuman scream. Nashala and the lion both turned around to see a great beast stomp out of the trees. It stopped screaming, but its rumbling growls were no less terrifying. It was gray like an angry sky, with white tusks that could skewer three men. Its eyes were small and fierce and its giant ears flapped aggressively. It was an elephant: the mother of the two calves.

The lion's bravado melted instantly as it bolted away as fast as its four legs could carry it; it appeared to be flying more than running. Nashala swallowed as the elephant approached her. The elephant's growling had ceased, but she still appeared tense, not sure if this strange animal was a threat to her children.

Nashala's nerves of steel were what prevented her from running away screaming from an animal that was a foot taller than her. Her reason for coming had run away, but she stared at the very thing that could best it. She had never even heard of anyone who had the soul of an elephant. With this, her family could rule forever. She'd be more powerful than anyone thought possible. But she had trained for a lion, not an elephant. It was feasible she wouldn't make it out alive.

She turned to the calves, huddled next to one another.

And even if she did, she wasn't sure if she could murder the elephant right in front of her children.

She turned back to the elephant. She tried to think of what her mother would do. She shakily took an arrow out and readied it, pointing it toward the elephant's eye. Her hand shook. What would her mother do?

Nashala remembered endurance training with her father, when she didn't think she could run another foot. She had doubled over, panting, wondering "What would my mother do," the pain of her lungs similar to the pain of her heart.

She remembered her father grabbing a fistful of her hair, her hair that was no longer there.

"She'd toss away the chance you've been given," she heard her father say.

Whatever her feelings, Nashala thought it was too late to turn away.

So, she let the arrow fly.

Many years have passed since the day when the young woman decided to challenge the elephant. Some who tell the tale give the name of the woman, out of respect. Others forego it. They argue her identity doesn't matter. It could happen to anyone. Besides, she ceased to be she that day.

After a long, grueling battle, the woman got exactly what she wanted. Mixed with the horrified screams of its children, the elephant cow fell with a cry. The woman took its soul. Then she screamed and writhed as her mind felt as if it were melting, as the stronger soul took over her body. And so, the elephant rose in her new body and went to comfort her children.

No one taking the Seizing travels in too far, because there are rumors of a wild woman who defends the inner jungle of Shana, mercilessly attacking humans. A woman with the body of a human, but the soul of a great elephant. The body of a woman who wished to be chief of humans, but came to be the chief of the animals.

TRADE

Kaleb A. Brown

My human has been gone for a while, but I know he'll be back because he loves me. He'll come back like he always does. My human will fill my bowl with food to stop my tummy from rumbling. He does it two times: when the ball in the sky is going up and it gets light in The Outside and when it's going down and it gets dark. Sometimes my human carries an entire package of food from The Outside in his big, strong arms! That's how I know he's the boss of the place; the boss is the one who gets the food, right? When I was a kitten, my mom gave me food, but ever since I've lived here, my human has been the one feeding me. At first, I thought he was my mom, but he's way too bald and clumsy to be another cat.

Earlier, I played on the structure my human made for me a bit, but it got boring after a while (though hearing the bell jangle is always fun), so now I'm just lying low in the basement, waiting for my human to get back. I love walking around the basement. It feels nice and cool on my paws. Upstairs it's always soft, so it's good for scratching but not so good for walking. I also love it 'cause my human doesn't clean the basement so there's always boxes to climb through and new things to find. Like those wriggly little black things with eight legs! I've gotten good at catching 'em. My human doesn't seem to like when I bring them to him though. He always makes a loud, high noise and shakes around.

My human is such a nice human. When I want to, he always lets me snuggle next to him, but he also lets me have alone time when I want. He doesn't mind if I spend all the time when the sky ball is up just roaming the house. He's a smart human, because everyone knows cats need cat time.

The humans I knew when I was a kitty weren't as smart or nice. Even though I had a perfectly good mom that could look after me, they still felt the need to constantly watch me. It really stressed me out.

But I'm okay now! Just kind of hungry. I'll just take a quick nap while I wait for him. I jump up from box to box until I'm nice and high up. If anything skitters across the floor, I'll see it and wake right up. But for now, it's nap time.

When I close my eyes, it's dark for a bit, but then my human will play with me before he goes out when the sky ball rises. It's super fun playing together. He dangles a bundle of feathers and a jingly thing in the air above my face. I try to catch it but he moves it away. I'm getting better, though. More and more, I pounce on it and wrestle with it before he can move it away.

I'm back in the basement and my ears perk up once I hear a sound from The Outside. It's a big rumbly sound about fifty paces (twenty-five if I run) to the left of the big room in the front of the domain. I know that sound! In about three paces of time, the rumbling sound will stop and there will be a clicking sound five paces after that.

Seven paces of time later: the rumbling stops.

Sixteen paces of time after that: a clicking sound.

I jump off the box and begin running up the basement stairs. The cool air quickly gets warmer. I turn and slide a bit on the floor. He's back! My human is back! In the big front room, I jump onto the ledge and move in front of the red sheet. I look out of the invisible wall to The Outside. In the wall, I can see a cat right in front of my face. It's so annoying. He's there every time I go to the invisible wall. One of his eyes is blue and the other is green. His fur is the color of the white stuff that falls from the sky when it's cold. This cat shows up everywhere, but he doesn't have a smell. What a weirdo.

Back to my human. He has some things in his hands. He's walking slower. He looks tired. I wait for him, following him with my eyes. I run to the Gate to The Outside once I hear metal jingling and look up. My eyes go wide as I see my human wearing the brown thing on his head and his brown, seasonal fur.

I start talking to him. Obviously, we speak different languages, so he doesn't really understand what I'm trying to say. Sometimes he seems to, though, so I always think it's at least worth a shot.

"Hello! I'm so happy to see you again, human," I say.

He doesn't say anything, just puts his bags down and closes the gate, shooing away the sky ball's light. His breathing is heavy.

I tilt my head. That's weird. Maybe he didn't hear me. Humans are funny like that. They have small, furless ears, so I don't think they can hear that well.

"Hello! I'm so happy to see you," I say again, but this time louder, raising my head high. Since I have his attention anyway, I add, "Food time!" He still doesn't say anything, just blows the breath the way humans do when they're tired, annoyed, or thinking about something.

I press against his legs. "Hello! I'm so—!"

He finally begins speaking. The only thing I can understand is my name. "Meow meow meow meow, Kris."

My human begins walking toward the back of the domain. No petting? I follow him as he walks further back. Hey, he's not going to the basement! I ram into the back of his thick legs, bumping my head against them. "Hey! Hey," I say.

"Meow meow," he says in his cute human language that's more annoying than cute right about now. He just keeps walking away from the basement into the room in the back, the room where he sleeps in his comfy box. He lies down and starts looking at his colorful square. I get between him and the square and nudge him. "Feed me, please," I say. "Come on, you have to—"

My fur stands rigid and I jump away from him as his entire body shakes and he lets out a noise from his mouth. I stare at him, scared, as he continues to do this, grabbing at his chest. I follow him as he leaves the room and goes to the small room with the human litter box he trained me to use. He keeps making the noise from his mouth. Soon, it smells like metal and there's some red stuff coming from his mouth. He wipes it away with a cloth and he stumbles away.

I go to the room in the front and lie down on the comfy box. I start scratching it. This usually gets his attention because he doesn't like when I do this and he always shoos me off. Not this time though. It sounds like he's drinking water.

It seems like he's forgotten about feeding me, but he's not a bad human. I still love him. Humans can just be silly sometimes. After all, if they weren't silly, they wouldn't trip over cats. As silly and clumsy as he can be, he's a lot nicer than the humans I used to know. They were just plain mean.

I was born with two sisters. At first, I couldn't see or hear anything, but even in the dark, I could feel my mom taking care of me. It's funny, but I think I liked the world better when I couldn't see or hear anything. I guess the humans don't bother you if you're small enough.

I was excited when I could finally see. The dark became light. A very, very bright light. It was so blurry that it hurt. No matter where I tried to move my head, I couldn't get away from the brightness. Everything was blurry and scary. My eyes weren't as good as they are now, so I couldn't make the room darker. I just closed my eyes and cried. My mom must have heard me and began licking and snuggling me. That made me feel better.

Soon, I was able to walk around a bit, but I was clumsy like my human. My sisters were, too. I could open my eyes without being hurt, but I didn't like the room. It was just a bright white room. If they didn't have blue eyes, I'm sure I wouldn't be able to see my sisters either. After walking around the room for a bit, I was bored. Once you've walked around a tiny room with nothing in it twice—once to see what it has, twice to see that it still doesn't have anything in it—I had seen it all. It stunk, but I'd have to stay there for a long time. I have no idea how long because I couldn't see the sky. I just know I was born there and left when I was big.

I first started seeing the humans when I began walking. They wore all white like the room and wore blue masks that covered their mouths. When I first saw them, I was excited. I thought they'd be new people to play with. Soon, I never wanted to see them again. They'd take me out, carry me down a long hallway, and then put me in a dark, cold room with a long white table. They'd poke my tummy with a sharp thing. They'd fill me with something, and then I'd get woozy. Everything would go dark. I'd wake up back in the White Room, feeling super tired.

They'd take my sisters out of the room, too. When they brought them back, my sisters would be asleep for a very long time. When they woke up, they staggered around as they walked.

We would keep asking mom when we could leave. Mom never said anything when we asked her this.

Whenever the humans would come to get me, they'd say something that sounded like "Kay-ar-fef-tene."

I remember the last day I saw my mom. One day, the humans decided to take me and my sisters at the same time. "Kay-ar-fef-tene." "Jay-ar-fef-tene." "El-ar-fef-tene." They scooped us up and brought us to the room. They did something different this time. The sharp thing looked a bit different. It hurt a lot when they brought it to my stomach and I screamed. My sisters did too. We tried to get away but the humans were so much bigger and stronger than us. I remember seeing a bit of red on the table. I still don't know what it is but now that I think about it, the red that my human had on his mouth reminded me of the red I saw that day.

The humans brought us over to The White Room and closed the gate to the hallway. Our mother ran over and started licking us, but no matter how much she did it, it didn't help us feel better. Okay, well maybe it made my heart feel a bit better and not my tummy feel better. Things started to get dark and me and my sisters fell down. Before it went completely black we kept crying, telling mom that we were scared.

I woke up. I felt fine. I remember feeling silly for being so scared. Mom was sleeping. I tried telling her that I was okay, but she wouldn't wake up. We tried nudging her, but no matter what we tried, she just slept. She didn't make sounds like she usually did when she was asleep. She felt cold. Something was wrong, but we didn't have anyone to turn to, only her.

We turned around as a human walked through the gate.

"Hey, our mom won't wake up!"

"Our mom's sick!"

"Please, you have to help her!"

The human just looked at a brown board that he carried and nodded his head. He said something I couldn't understand. I still remember it because I remember everything that day. It sounded like "suk-ses." He took my mom away and I never saw her again. Later, they'd take my sisters away. I was all alone.

They continued taking me to the room and poking me with the sharp thing. A few times, they'd bring me to the room and put me in a metal box with holes in it. In the box with me was one of those singing, flying things that I see outside. It didn't move. It reminded me of my mom. I was scared and cried, begging for the humans to let me out. When they'd finally take me out, they'd yell at me before taking me back to the room.

I hated it there and I never thought I'd leave.

Then I met my human.

One day, another human came in, and I moved away from him like I always do. Since he was so much bigger than me, he scooped me up. When we went down the hall, though, he didn't go in the room. We kept walking. My chest felt tight. Were we leaving? Could I see my mom again? Soon, we were in a giant place where the air felt nice and I could hear a million sounds. We were in The Outside, and after being stuck in the White Room for so long, it was the most beautiful thing ever. I still go to the invisible wall and stare at it, appreciating it for showing me that things aren't all bad.

My human put me in his rumbling box and we moved away from the White Room, far far away, deep into The Outside. We went to many places before he took me to the Domain I know and love. I'm happy that he saved me. He's so nice and I love him so much.

So I'm not too mad that he's not feeding me. He must have a good reason. I'll just close my eyes for a bit and when I open them, there'll be food in my bowl.

***

Nope, not even a piece. I'm pretty annoyed now. Good human or not, he's being just plain scatterbrained. What if I kept him from eating? I'm sure he wouldn't like it. Of course, he can feed himself, I can't. I used to be able to; my human used to put the food box next to my bowl. Whenever I wanted extra food, I'd knock it over and eat the food that spilled out. Now he puts the food high up behind a human door that you can't open with cat paws, only human paws.

I walk all across the basement perking my ears up. Maybe if I'm lucky, I can find a mouse to eat. I tell myself that food's tastier when you have to catch it. I turn my head upwards as I hear my human walk, putting something in the trash box. I race up the stairs. I tell myself that food's tastier when you don't have to catch it. I sniff once I get near the trash box. Yup, food. Smells like a lot of meat. Yum. I jump up and knock the trash box over before dragging out the food. It's one of the jumbo food things he always gets. It has like three different kinds of meat, some plants, and white sauce and brown sauce. Though now it also has some red sauce on it. It tastes kind of funny, it's a very strong taste and it's kind of thick. Oh well, it's food.

I nibble on the meat, thinking about how weird it is. My human never wastes food, but it seems like he barely ate this. It looks like he took one bite and that's where the red sauce is. Forgetting to feed me, throwing away food, it's not like him at all. Maybe he's sick.

When I'm done eating, I wait outside the room with the litter box. It sounds like he's getting the Hot Rain, again. I hear him make the same loud noise as before. I decide to go to his room and wait on his comfy box. Maybe I can make him feel better.

He's out of the litter room soon and coming into the room slowly. His eyes look tired and I can hear him breathing. He's definitely sick. I'm worried. I wonder what will happen if he doesn't get better. I stop thinking about it; there's no point in thinking such sad thoughts. Of course, my human will get better.

My human smiles (humans are cute when they smile) when he sees me. "Meow meow meow Kris." I'm glad he's not too sick to talk to me. The day my human stops talking to me is the day he stops being my human; he'd just be like the other humans I knew, the mean ones.

He makes the noise again and his entire body shakes. I just sit there on the comfy box. I won't run away. If I'm not scared, he won't be scared, and if he isn't scared then maybe he'll get better. Maybe that's why my mom didn't get better, because we were all scared.

He turns off the lights, so I have to let my eyes adjust to the dark as he scoots in the comfy box, looking at his colorful square. I just let him be, maybe it will help him feel better.

He makes the sound again.

Maybe not.

I'm at his feet so I can feel a bit of it through him. I can't imagine being in his place.

His breathing is even louder now. I'm keeping calm. I hear the sound of him turning the colorful box off. He drops it to the ground. There's a soft patting sound near the fluffy thing he puts his head on; he's patting the space, telling me that he wants me to come. I stand up and move to the space. I'm keeping calm.

I sigh once he puts his hand on my head, slowly moving it down to the end of my back, making my fur and skin feel good. I purr because I can't help it.

"Meow, meow," he says.

He makes the sound again and it takes all the strength I have not to jump. I move closer to him, right next to his head. He continues petting me, talking quietly. His breath smells like the red sauce earlier. He's talking a lot and I just really wish he could speak cat or I could speak human or just anything that would help us talk to each other. Because I haven't a clue what he's saying, but I bet it's nice. I bet he's saying he's sorry for not feeding me, that he's sorry for scaring me with his noise (except I'm not scared, like I said), and that I'm a good friend. Or at least I hope that's what he's saying.

His breathing gets quieter and quieter, his petting gets slower and slower. Soon, the petting stops. I can't hear his breath even though it was so loud before. I turn to him. He's smiling. I want to think that he's sleeping, but something feels wrong. When cats and humans sleep, you can still hear them breathe. It doesn't seem like he's sleeping. It seems like he's sleep.

"Human? Human, wake up." I move from his hand, which falls to the bed. I lick his face, but he doesn't react. He usually giggles and wakes up. "Human?"

I feel bad, but I'm out of options. I take my claws out and scratch his arm. Just a bit, to wake him up. As I drag down, I see red marks on his arm. But he's still. I was supposed to be calm, but I think I have permission to freak out now.

"Wake up," I cry, jumping on his chest. When I do, I want to go limp. The thing that beats in his chest is gone. It's not there anymore. Why is it not there? That doesn't make any sense. It's always there, even when he's sleeping.

I jump up and down on him. I scratch him some more. I do everything, crying, trying to make him wake up, but nothing works. I want to call to someone, tell them my human won't wake up, that he's sick, that they have to help him. But there's no one but me.

I lie down on his chest, waiting for the beat that will never come.

Heart, that's what it is. His heart is gone. And there's nothing I can do about it.

I remember my mom and how she was sick, how I couldn't do anything to help her.

Then I realize how she helped me before.

Me and my sisters were sick. My mom came to us and when we woke up, we were fine and she was sick. She took our sickness for us, because she cared about us. I think I can do it too. That's why the humans put me in boxes with other sick things.

I look at my human's smiling face. I'm not scared. Knowing he won't wake up if I don't help him is scarier. It's funny; he's so much bigger than me. He taught me how to use the human litter, he feeds me, and he brought me all the way here from the white room. But here I am, not even as big as his leg, yet I'm going to save him.

It makes me feel good.

I stand up on his chest and close my eyes. I think about all the times we shared, all the playing and laughing. I think about how grateful I am to him. Then I start to feel hot.

Not like warm and fuzzy (though I feel that, too), but actually hot, like burning. It hurts. But I can start to feel his heart through his chest. I fall, my chest growing tight, while hoping his grows light. I start to feel him breathing again. That's good.

My human has been gone for a while, but I know he'll be back because I love him. He'll come back like he always does. I hope he thinks about me every day, when the sky ball is going up and when the sky ball is going down.

BLACK ODYSSEY

Kaleb A. Brown

Beyond the visor of my spacesuit, I'm greeted by the sight of darkness. Past the border that separates my thoughts from the world at large is the sound of silence. Save for the beating of my heart and the feeling of my breath leaving my nose and lips, there is no evidence of life. In the darkness, there is no evidence of any form of existence besides my own. In this abyss, I'm not confident that anything will be here after I go. As far as I can tell, the world ends with me.

I've done a lot of thinking here, because my thoughts are the only company I have left. My thoughts chastise me, saying that I took basic, primal things for granted. Things like a sense of self. Whenever I'm starting to forget who I am, I list essential information: what city I'm from, what planet I was born to, what solar system and galaxy I call home, my Cosmological Pilot rank. However, the more I forget to list off, the less I ground myself, the more I seem to forget who I am, become one with the void.

Part of my problem is that I'm missing two of the Fundamental Perceptions of Sapience: a sense of time and a sense of space.

I have no idea where I am. Fleeing Betelgeusian pirates, I did the first thing they teach you not to do during Basing Cosmology Training: I went into an unmarked wormhole. My lightspeeder disappeared into the uncharted swirl of light, and when I emerged from the hole, my speedster jolted to a halt, nearly sending me through the front of my craft. I quickly discovered the problem—wherever my speeder dropped me is completely lightless. I've been looking this entire time and there isn't a solitary star.

What fills me with dread isn't the darkness, though— children are taught to fight their primal fear of the dark. They are, however, encouraged to make a fuss if they're lost. This place has no universal coordinates. This place couldn't be tracked on my MultiNav. Fine, that makes sense—a wormhole wouldn't be unmarked for long if its destination spot was known, but the MultiNav won't even tell me what I'm near. I could be one hundred billion or one hundred trillion miles away from Andromeda. I tried radioing someone, anyone, but the signal is just devoured by the silence. Don't ask me how, but I swear this place doesn't have the Cosmic Background Radiation. For these reasons, I've been calling this place The Dead Zone. That name is going to take on a much grimmer meaning.

I have no idea what time it is. I arrived here Day 163.5, Year 013C per the Standard Andromedan Calendar. Even as state-of-the-art as this one is, lightspeeders aren't built to sustain people for extended durations, so even though I used low settings, the ship had power for a week before systems shut off. Now the only thing keeping me alive is my suit. Wanting to save power, I shut down all unnecessary functions. That included the watch. Time in complete darkness, in complete mystery, might as well not exist. There are times when I feel like I've been here only for a little over a week since my speeder died, and other times it feels like I've been here for months.

Everything is a guess. Guessing what day it could possibly be. Guessing how much sustenance I have left. Guessing who I am. Guessing if this is reality or if this is just a nightmare that I can't escape from.

I'm talking to myself and recording this because I fear I'll go mad if I don't. No color, no shapes, no sight. No sound but the sound of my voice and the buzzing of my thoughts. I know it's a waste of air, but sometimes I scream just to make sure I'm there. At times, I fear that I've died and just haven't realized it yet.

My mind has begun to play tricks on me. Every so often, I hear voices in the distance. I get hopeful before realizing it's just my imagination. I can tell because if I stop and focus, I realize they're voices I recognize—parents, past friends, lovers, celebrities. They're just so distant that they're always indistinct once I start to hear them. I wonder if they're okay. I wonder if they'll remember me. I wonder if they really matter, floating out here in darkness. I wonder how my world is getting by now that I'm gone. If they're doing just fine, perhaps I have no right to call it my world at all. Maybe my world is contained in the confines of this suit and this mind. If that's the case, what a dismal world I find myself in.

I wish I knew what day it was. I wish I knew with confidence the day I cracked. In the distance, I see a hazy brightness. It's so dim that I struggle to even call it light. It's more like the memory of light. But still, it's something and it shifts slightly as I move. If I close my eyes, it's gone. But I can still feel it there, beckoning to me. Then there's the voices. I'm sure I'm not imagining things because these aren't voices I've heard before, at least not like this. I hear children laughing, bells ringing, and a choir. The "light" is beginning to pulse. I think I'm going to go to the light.

I thought I'd never break one of the most basic Basic Cosmology Training rules: Never take off your suit in space. If you have the desire to, they warned, you're most likely suffering from space sickness. Maybe I am. Maybe I've been deprived so long that I'll do anything if I believe it will get me closer to the warmth of a living being. I can't hear the bells clearly with this helmet on. I can't feel the warmth of the light with this suit on. If I'm really sick, out here, alone, then there's no helping me, I might as well be on the move and then let myself waste away. So, consequences be damned, I'm taking this thing off so I can properly start the world, my world. Because even though I'm not certain I'll live if I go forward without my suit, I'm certain I'll die if I just sit here. Nothing will happen if I don't move. As far as I can tell, the world begins with me.

THE ARCHAEOLOGIST

L.L. Renno

In the Great Valley, the past was waiting to be unmasked.

The Archaeologist looked over the work that had happened in front of him. They had uncovered a city. A great city, one that was likely a center for culture and art countless eons ago. It had been buried under a thick layer of dirt and rubble until a mere few days ago, when it had finally been uncovered.

As the Archaeologist surveyed the newly discovered sight, his Student crept up beside him.

"Do you think this was built by the Ancients as well, sir?" the Student asked.

"Yes indeed, my dear boy. In fact, this may have been one of their greatest achievements," the Archaeologist replied.

The Archaeologist walked amongst the ruins for a while, taking in the surroundings. There were destroyed towers covered in broken sheets of glass, with pathways wide enough for twenty humans to stand side by side, the walls covered in intricate markings. Once there must have been noise. But now there were only the soft footsteps of the two scholars.

"Just look at the complex construction of these buildings, or the precise engineering of these roads," the Archaeologist said. "Look at all this incredible technological expertise! We were not able to achieve such exquisite craftsmanship until just a little over a century ago!"

"It's truly wonderful, sir," the Student mumbled.

While the Archaeologist admired the great structures around him, he instead chose a humble tenement as his first place to inspect personally.

The Student noticed this about him and others in his field: the Archaeologist always said that he found the smaller things far more interesting than the grand and opulent constructions most other less learned individuals lusted after.

Within the tenement, the Archaeologist stopped in front of a skeleton. A human skeleton. Two human skeletons, in fact. It was a sight that the Student was used to, but nevertheless it unnerved him ever so slightly.

"By the looks of it, they died rather slowly," the Archaeologist said quietly.

They were propped against the wall, seated and leaning against each other.

"I have seen this exact same situation in every single ruin I have excavated. Lovers, sharing a final moment before their ends. These were clearly a people that cared deeply for each other. It causes one to wonder how they died out."

"Do you have any ideas, sir?"

"Well, the most commonly accepted theory is some kind of monumental natural disaster. Rapid climate change caused by volcanism, perhaps. Or maybe a meteorite. Perhaps even a gamma-ray burst from a nearby supernova. Of course, there are other ideas, such as that ridiculous theory that the old fool I share space with has been peddling."

"You mean the one where the Ancients wiped themselves out?"

"Indeed. The damn simpleton believes that the Ancients changed the environment of this world in a way that made it uninhabitable. I keep telling him: How could a civilization so advanced and intelligent be foolish enough to cause its own extinction? Aside from the lack of obvious evidence that their doom was caused by anything other than something natural, I have never heard of any society being so reckless! But the man sticks to his theory. He never listens."

"Such is life, I suppose," the Student said.

"Indeed, such is life," the Archaeologist replied. "Such is life."

END OF THE CENTURY

L.L. Renno

It's a beautiful day.

I lean back in my favorite rocking chair, watching the sun creep toward the horizon, igniting the sky around it. A warm breeze is coming, sending ripples like waves on the ocean shore across the patchy lawn. I wait patiently, watching the road in front of me, listening for the telltale crunching of gravel that lets me know my granddaughter is coming home from school.

Something passes down the road, but it's gone before I have a chance to take in its details. I see what it left behind: a familiar, tightly rolled bundle of papers. I get out of my rocking chair to retrieve my weekly dose of news, walking stick in hand as I limp ahead. Bending down, I feel a sudden pain in my back. It's a common occurrence, though with the weight of my life on my shoulders, I often find myself surprised that I can even walk at all.

Once I'm settled back in my rocking chair, I unfurl the bundle to read the weekly edition of The New York Times. For the most part, there are no surprises. A presidential candidate outlining his promises, apparently under the delusion that whatever skeleton government still exists in Washington even matters anymore. An update on a war between distant countries I can't even place on a map. The weather forecast for the next week. And, of course, the results of last Monday's football game. I suppose some things never really change.

I set the papers aside, looking out to the empty houses, barely visible through the trees that surround my house. There used to be people who lived in them, but most have decided to move closer to the town center, to tenements that are not quite as nice, but are less vulnerable to attacks from bandits. Though just beyond the houses there is a steel fence—topped with wicked coils of barbed wire—that stops all but the most determined bandits, most prefer not to take any chances. I suppose I'm stubborn for not joining them, or maybe I'm just too old to be afraid of brigands anymore.

My granddaughter's taking longer to come home than usual. I try not to think much of it. This is hardly the first time she's been this late, but part of me cannot help but worry. These days, death—especially the sudden variety—is common enough to not be worth much more than a passing thought. Infection, cholera, malnutrition, murder at the hands of bandits, provoking the garrison—I've seen it all. Sometimes I wonder how I've avoided it this long. I'm easily the oldest person in our community and some of my granddaughter's friends believe I'm the oldest person on Earth, which I can't help but doubt. At least I don't want to believe that's true.

I hear the crunching of gravel again, though I can tell it's not my granddaughter. The sound is slower, inconsistent, clearly produced by someone on foot. I get up from my rocking chair again and limp toward the end of my property, intending to meet whoever's approaching.

I make eye contact with him as soon as he reaches my mailbox. I recognize him as Will, a member of the local garrison. He's a young man, scarcely older than my granddaughter, with black hair cut extremely short and a cloak of stubble enclosing the lower half of his face. He's wearing an old army uniform that's cut and torn in various places, and he's got an assault rifle slung over his shoulder. For a moment, I wonder why he's here, but then I remember: Today's the day the monthly protection tax is collected.

"Good day, Mrs. Lee," Will says as soon as I'm close enough. "I do hope you're ready to pay for our protection this month. Five Silver Dollars, I believe, or the equivalent of that amount in food or material objects."

"I was under the impression we don't owe anything," I tell him. "I believe General McGowan gave us a special exemption."

Will frowns.

"Now that you mention it, I do believe he said something like that. Something about him and your son being tight?"

I don't say anything. The memories are too painful.

"Knowing the general, though, his charity ain't gonna last forever. I suppose you're lucky you don't have many years left in you. Otherwise, he'd probably just banish you like the others who're too old and weak to work."

Ignoring his sneer, my attention is drawn to the sound of an approaching bicycle.

Soon, my granddaughter pulls to a stop next to me. Her hair, tied into a loose, messy knot, is the color of coffee like her mother's, but straight and coarse like her father's. She's dressed in her usual outfit, one of my old moth-eaten T-shirts, a tattered pair of her mother's old jeans, her grandfather's hoodie, and her father's canvas messenger bag. In short, she's a perfect echo of our family.

My granddaughter dismounts from her bike. As soon as Will sees her, his attitude changes. That sneer vanishes in an instant, and his eyes dart to the side nervously.

"Hey Will, what're you doing here?" she asks.

"Nothing, Hazel," Will replies. "Your grandmother and I were just exchanging pleasantries. If you'll excuse me, I'll continue my patrol."

With that, Will nods tersely to both of us before running further down the road. My granddaughter, arms crossed under her chest, gives his retreating back a withering look.

"I'm guessing he was asking you for payment again?" she asks me. I nod, and she shakes her head.

"Hopeless. Just hopeless. Will's always had a terrible memory for this sort of thing. Almost makes you wonder how he even remembers his patrol route."

I decide to change the subject. "How was your day?" I ask.

"Well," Hazel says, "it was all right. I'll tell you more after I put my stuff down."

"All right, all right," I say, not bothering to restrain the hint of a smile I feel escaping across my face. "How about I make some tea?"

"Sounds great, Grandma!" Hazel says, beaming at me and running ahead. I take a moment to admire her energy before I limp back toward the house.

Ascending the porch steps, I walk through the flaking white door into the entrance hall. A door to the right leads to the messy kitchen with its salvaged appliances and worn wooden table and chairs. From one of the nearly empty cupboards, I take out my prized porcelain teapot—one of the few things I still have from my old life—and two simple ceramic mugs. From another cupboard, I withdraw my rusted iron kettle and a small bundle of local herbs—I haven't been able to find proper tea in years—and I set them on the counter. After filling the kettle with water from my sink, I place it on my hot plate and turn it on.

The water takes more time than I'd like to boil, but I temper my impatience by reminding myself of my fortune. Most small settlements like this one don't even have the luxury of running water or reliable electricity. This minor miracle was my son's doing. He somehow managed to fix the old infrastructure so that it functioned again, at least in a limited capacity. It isn't completely normal, but it's better than going back to the Dark Ages. It doesn't take much to wonder why General McGowan was so fond of him.

The telltale whistle lets me know the water has come to a boil. I turn off the hot plate and drop the herbs into my teapot, followed by boiling water from the kettle. I wait a moment or two for the "tea" to steep.

Both ceramic mugs in one hand, I return to the porch, where Hazel's already sitting on the steps waiting for me. I settle down next to her, motioning for her to grab one of the mugs from my trembling hand. "As Hazel takes small sips of the scalding liquid, I ask about her day.

"Well," Hazel begins, "I have this annoying essay I have to write for History. One and a half pages explaining the Militia Authorization Act and its effects on the fundamental structure of American society. Due next Monday."

"One and a half pages?" I say. "You have no idea how lucky you've got it, do you?"

"Come on, Grandma," she says, "you know I'm no good at writing."

"I know, I know," I say. "Don't worry. I'll help you with it later."

"Thanks," Hazel says. "On the bright side, we've been working on setting up for the Centennial Festival recently. Sarah found a box full to the brim with old smartphones and we're thinking of emptying the cases and replacing the insides with drawings of a bunch of different scenes from the past century. Maybe even putting on some kind of raffle or auction to raise money for the school. We're not sure yet."

I stay silent for a moment. I have almost forgotten that the end of the century is only a few weeks away. It will be the conclusion of the only century I've ever known, and yet it feels like it shouldn't be over yet. Then again, if there is one thing I've learned in the history classes that I now barely remember, the past two centuries have not been lacking in rapid change. It seems only natural that the end of this century would be unrecognizable from that of the last.

"Are you okay, Grandma?" my granddaughter asks, snapping me out of my thoughts.

"Oh," I say. "Yes, I'm all right. Is there anything else that happened today?"

"Well..." Hazel trails off. Suddenly, her demeanor changes, eyes darting, voice stuttering. I'm confused. It's not like her to get nervous in this way, so I worry about what might've happened.

"You know Alex?" Hazel finally manages to say.

"Was he that kid who got into hot water with General McGowan after he accidentally shot a hole in the water tower a few months ago?" I ask, straining my memory.

"No, Grandma, you're thinking of Ollie," Hazel replies, appalled but laughing. "Alex is that guy you met at the Halloween gala last year, remember? The one who wore that worn-out dinosaur costume."

At Hazel's description, the face of a weathered, but strangely handsome young man surfaces in my mind.

"Of course," I say, "what about him?"

"The thing is..." she says, hesitating, "he asked me out."

Relief sweeps over me like a splash of warm water. Of course, it's boys that are making her nervous. And here I was worried it was something to actually be concerned about. It gives me pause, makes me remember a time all those years ago when I helped my son with his own courtship struggles. Or even further back, when I myself was the naive young girl infatuated with a boy I barely knew anything about.

"And what did you say?" I ask her.

"I said yes, I'd love to," Hazel said. "We're meeting at the park tonight, and I'm not sure what to do. Like, what do I wear? How should I act? Nobody's ever asked me out before, oh God, what am I supposed to do?"

I can't help but chuckle a little.

"Grandma!" she says, blushing.

"Sorry, I know I shouldn't laugh. This is something everybody goes through. I had a similar experience when I first met your grandfather."

"What do you suggest I do then?"

"Well," I say, "this'll likely sound rather cliché, but the truth is, you can only be yourself. Most people can tell if you aren't being genuine and even if they buy into it, you'll still have to spend considerable time and effort putting up a facade that isn't you."

"If, however," I continue, "If he doesn't treat you right..." I curl my hand into a fist and make a motion in the air. "You've got my permission to slug him right in the face!"

Hazel laughs at this. "Grandma, that's awful!"

"All right, maybe you shouldn't hit him. Only if he tries to do something terrible. Which I hope he doesn't."

"He won't," she says. "I know him well enough to know he'd never do anything like that. Well, at least on purpose."

Hazel finishes the last of her tea.

"Thanks, Grandma. I think I'll go get ready now. He wants to meet up with me in an hour or so."

"All right then," I say. "Tell you what, don't worry about what to wear. I'll find something that'll suit you perfectly."

Smiling, she nods, and heads back into the house. I wait for a few moments before following her up the stairs to the top floor. Through one of the doors is my dusty bedroom, with a closet I haven't bothered to open in years. It's mostly full of my old clothes, pieces that no longer fit me, or things I've had no occasion to wear. At least, until now.

The doors open with a creak, and I poke through my old things until I find what I'm looking for. Taking out one of the several nondescript black garment bags, I unzip it to reveal its contents. It's a beautiful mint-green summer dress, the same one that I wore on my first date with the man who'd eventually become my husband all those years ago. I take it from its hiding place deep within the closet and run my fingers across the fabric, absorbing all the memories it holds.

Setting the dress down on my bed, I notice something else on the floor of the closet. Limping back over, I kneel down and pick it up, turning it over in my hands. What I see almost makes me lose control of my emotions.

I recognize the photograph from a New Year's party seventeen years ago. A group of people, standing in a Manhattan loft, stare back at me. I look at their faces. First, I see myself, still elderly, but in far better health than I am now. Next to me, my husband David, who would pass away peacefully in his sleep a mere month after this picture was taken. Then my daughter-in-law Rose, youthful and healthy, showing no traces of the consumptive plague that would take her before Hazel was even a year old. And finally, my son, one arm around his wife, and another around a bundle of blankets, within which a small, pale face is scarcely visible. He still looks so handsome in this photo, no signs of the wound he left in his skull from his final attempt to reunite with the love of his life.

I think back to the city we all left behind. When we lived there, many still considered it the greatest city in the world. Even when we abandoned it for the countryside, as the oceans were reclaiming it street by street, building by building, it was still home to hundreds of thousands of people. I've only heard rumors about what it's like now, an eerie ghost town, home to only a small group of desperate refugees and stubborn stragglers.

Once again, it's Hazel, my granddaughter, the only family I have left, who brings me back into reality. I hear the splashing from her bathing coming from nearby. I take one last look at the picture before putting it on my end table. Picking the dress back up, I walk into Hazel's room.

I don't have to wait long before she exits the ragtag bathroom with a towel wrapped around her. I help her put the dress on, and afterwards, I fix her hair, tying it into the elaborate knot that I used to wear in my youth. She stands up to look at herself in the dusty mirror, admiring every angle.

"It's perfect," Hazel finally says.

I walk her down the stairs to the front porch. By now, the sun's dipped completely below the horizon, and the sky has bathed itself in more stars than I've seen in my old life. I suppose there's a silver lining to living at the end of civilization.

"Are you sure you don't want me to walk with you to the park?" I say.

"No thanks. I know how to get there. And I think you should get some rest. You've done a lot for me today."

My granddaughter prepares to go down the steps, but then she remembers something. She turns back and throws her arms around me. Putting my own arms around her, I hold her close.

"I love you, Grandma," Hazel says, and with one last wave, she sets off down the porch steps and toward the road, soon disappearing into the night.

As I settle back down in my rocking chair, I can't help but wonder what the future holds for her. I certainly won't be around for much longer to see it, but a few things I know for sure. My granddaughter will likely never be able to learn to drive, go to college, or travel the world. She'll never know the frustration of being stuck in a traffic jam, or the rush to get a frozen espresso drink before work. She'll never have the life I had, but I can see, or at least I can hope, that in her own way she'll find happiness.

I lean back. It's been a beautiful day.

OUT OF THE SEA

Ivy Obuchowski

The salty ocean air called to me even when I was asleep. I'd been told time and time again to close my windows before going to bed, especially in the summer. Storms could appear at any time and blow in, ensuring that whatever I owned would be covered in seawater. Dad may have fixed up the old lighthouse to make it habitable for us, specifically me, but it wasn't a good place to add central air, so we had AC units in most windows. However, it would get so stuffy, I had to have my window open. Or maybe I felt too confined and had to rely on my parents to take me to the mainland because it was hard for me to get around on my own. Dad taught me how to operate a boat but I hadn't yet taken the boating test to get my license. I dreamed about that like my friends dreamed of getting their driver's license. For now, I had to watch storms and the horizon from high up in the lighthouse.

This storm was no different from most. Thunder boomed and I sat up, squinting against the harsh glare of my phone that proclaimed the time as seven-thirty in the morning. The curtains were dancing in the breeze and rain was coming in through the screen that cut the size of the water from droplets into mist. I let it hit my face for a second before I got up, using the nightstand and then the desk chair as a support.

Before I could close the window, I spotted a hazy light bouncing on the waves. Fishermen will often spend the night just offshore if they're too far from Bear Harbor where they sell their catch. Dad had put in a dock for them along the less rocky side of the island to moor their boats if a storm came up. I spent a lot of time there talking with them and asking questions about being out at sea. One had joked that I must be half mermaid or a selkie since I couldn't get enough of their stories.

I could barely see the lights at the end of the dock but the boat was a mile out at least and visibility was getting worse. Grabbing my binoculars, I leaned against the windowsill. I could make out two people on a small sloop trying to keep from capsizing, but they hadn't pulled their sails in. One good gust would send them into the sea. And who knew if they had a radio and were sending out an SOS.

The radio we kept on in the living room crackled but I couldn't hear whatever it was the person was saying through all the static. We always had the radio set to the fishermen's channel and most recreational boats use the same one. I limped as fast as I could out of my room and sat down at the table. Pulling the radio microphone closer to me with one hand, I slowly turned the tuning knob with the other. Dad had trained me on the radio when I was eight to take my mind off the surgery I had to correct my spina bifida. Now that I'm older, it's my official duty on the search and rescue team to man the radio.

After a minute, the message came through: "Help! We need help!"

"Unidentified craft, this is Carolynn. Over."

It was silent for what felt like a minute. Every second counts in this kind of situation. While I waited for a response, I kept hitting the bell you see on a hotel manager's desk over and over until I heard my dad rustle down the hall. "Unidentified craft, this is Carolynn. Over."

"Carolynn, my name is Charlie." A different voice responded. He sounded young and far calmer than the other voice. "Me and my dad aren't experienced sailors and can't get the sails in. The wind is getting stronger, over."

"Copy, stay calm. A rescue team will be sent out right away. Over and out."

I called Mr. Lowell, Dad's first mate as it were, and relayed the message. He would wake up George and Mark, the men I knew would be on call tonight. Next step was to switch on the light in the lighthouse proper that Dad couldn't bear to part with and only used when he went out with the team.

Dad barreled into the living room at full speed as I was making my way to the big switch labeled "Emergency," flipped said switch, and asked, "Is the team ready?"

"They should be here in two minutes," I said, standing. "Two people are on a recreational watercraft a mile out and can't get their sails in. Father and son, most likely on vacation."

He kissed the top of my head. "Thank you, love. Are you up for going out or do you want to stay here?"

"I'll go, the storm's not as bad as it was a few minutes ago."

"Meet us at the dock with the handheld?"

"It's my job."

The radio crackled again; Mr. Lowell and the rest of the crew were waiting for my dad at the dock. I strapped my crutches to my forearms and hobbled out after him with my kit thrown over my shoulder. Rain pelted my face as lightning streaked across the sky but I could tell that the sun was trying to rise over the horizon.

Dad practically jumped in the dinghy and sped off, leaving me waiting at the end of the dock. I may have been taught everything about working on a search and rescue team but I would only get in the way if I went out with them. It hurt, because I wanted to be on the water more than anything, but they needed someone to communicate with onshore and that was something I was good at. I set up my folding stool and pulled out the handheld radio.

"Charlie, this is Carolynn. Over."

"Carolynn, this is Charlie. Over."

"The rescue team is on their way out to you. Over."

He sighed before replying, "Copy that, I see 'em. Thank you, over and out."

In situations like these, time often seems to move slower than it actually is. I was able to monitor the team's progress with my binoculars while the storm was dying out and dark waves were whipping up. They would turn blue when the sunlight hit them and they reflected the blue wavelengths of light back into space. Right now, they were gray, black, and green with seaweed that had been ripped up from who knows where.

Eventually, I spotted the rescue dinghy on the crest of a wave with the sloop not far behind. The sloop had its sails pulled in and didn't appear to be damaged. As Charlie said, he and his dad weren't experienced, which made me wonder why they had decided to go out so early in the morning and not check the weather. Summer storms are common and crop up at any time but can also disappear as quickly as they came. Even with the emergency, I loved hearing the thunder roll over the ocean as the waves went up and onto the dock, soaking my pants and forcing me to stand.

By the time they pulled up to the dock with Mark at the sloop's helm, it felt like a half hour had gone by, though the watch I had stuffed in my pocket said I'd been awake for only ten minutes. Dad and George jumped out of the boat as Mr. Lowell kept one hand on the motor, telling a man with wild, windblown hair to stay put. I started to pack up my gear as a younger man, around seventeen or eighteen, attempted to jump to the sloop or the dock—I don't know what he was trying to do.

He fell into the ocean instead.

"Charlie!" The man dropped his suitcase and looked like he was going to go overboard himself but Mr. Lowell held him back. Dad had his hands full of rope; Mark was on the sloop throwing ropes to George to tie it off. I didn't know how good of a swimmer the kid was, but I did know there was a rip current close to the dock that looked like a zipper in the water where no waves were breaking. Charlie had jumped right into it.

I looked around. The men were busy and the kid was in danger of being swept further out to sea than where his boat was. He was trying to swim against the current, but that would only tire him out. I didn't notice if he was wearing a life jacket.

This was my chance.

With a glance at Dad, who was quickly untying the dinghy, I unstrapped my crutches, grabbed the life buoy, and jumped in. The clouds were breaking up and the sun properly rising to give me enough light to see Charlie's head and orange life jacket bobbing on the waves. He had given up on swimming and was yelling for help as he kept getting further and further away. I relished the feeling of cutting through the water, taking a breath as that odd wave crested in the rip current, and popping through the other side. Everything that held me back on dry land gave me power as I swam toward Charlie.

I reached him right as I heard Dad yell, "Carolynn, stay there! We'll come get you."

As much as I wanted to drag Charlie back to shore myself, I knew it would be taxing trying to stay in place and I had to obey orders. I ducked under the water and came back up in the middle of the ring. Sure, I could tread water for a while but I also wanted to keep ahold of the kid so they could pull us in at the same time. I grabbed onto the strap that tightens the belt around his waist. It should be enough to keep us together.

He had calmed down when he saw me next to him, looking less scared and somewhat impressed that I had jumped in after him. "Are you all right?" I asked.

"Shocked, is all. Nice to be able to put a face to the voice." Even though he was in a potentially life-threatening situation, his brown eyes were lit with laughter and life. "Do you make a habit of jumping into the ocean to rescue a stranger?"

"Only when that stranger tries to jump off the boat before it's tied up. Do you make a habit of doing stupid things like that?"

"Isn't what you did very stupid as well?"

I opened my mouth to retort but then Dad and Mr. Lowell came up in the boat. Mr. Lowell grabbed onto Charlie, hauling him up by his life jacket, while Dad reached under my arms and lifted me and the ring out of the water. Blankets were wrapped around us in a matter of seconds.

Charlie sat next to his dad and I sat next to mine. I could tell that Charlie was waiting for a scolding, for me to get in trouble for what I just did. Sure, he might not have been in much danger, having a life jacket and with the team still there, but that rip current was a pretty nasty one. I had been trained to escape it both with and without a life jacket but it was only on the third session with Mr. Lowell and Mark watching from the dinghy that I didn't panic. To not have control and glide through the water freaked me out, but it was important to feel that if things went wrong, I could handle it. Dad had insisted I learn so I would be prepared when I went out on my own.

Now, he clapped a hand on my shoulder and gave a little squeeze.

"Good work, Carolynn."

The kid's eyes widened as I turned to him and said, "I work the radio for the search and rescue team. How do you think I knew what I was talking about?"

"But that wasn't the radio, that was saving someone!"

"When everyone else is occupied, I'm allowed to jump in, so to speak, if it's within my ability to do so. And that's exactly what happened."

It was his turn to get cut off as we pulled up to the dock. George tossed a rope to Dad while Mr. Lowell sternly instructed Charlie to stay put this time.

Or we would let the ocean take him where it willed.

PAST LEARNING AND PRETENDING

Ivy Obuchowski

There are more people on the field and in the park than any Fourth of July I can remember. Everyone's here for the reenactment of the Battle of Lil' Ol' Hill, a small battle in a small town in West Virginia that occurred near the end of the Civil War. We've had reenactments before, but never on this scale. This one started as the final project for my history class at the community college and soon they had everyone in town endorsing it. The historical society I work for had to hire more people and find hundreds of volunteers. And of course, it was all Parker's idea.

"I never thought it would get this big, Lisbeth," he says, leaning against a tree, rifle forgotten on the ground and sleeves rolled up on his uniform. I'm still in jeans and the historical society T-shirt with a cardigan thrown on top of it. "I was just thinking about what it'd be like to recreate the battle as accurately as possible."

"Our teacher thought it was a brilliant idea." I brush the tree buds off of his cap, at least the ones I can reach. Parker's been tall since fifth grade when he had a growth spurt. Nearly ten years later, he's half a foot taller than I am, but he's still my lovable goofy nerd just like I'm his.

"Yeah, but look at all those people. Founders' Day isn't even this busy."

"Hey, this is something we've been talking about for years, remember? We wanted to see what it'd be like." I know Parker's not completely seeing me when he looks; what he sees is his sweetheart, the girl who'll wait for him until the war's over. The roles we play have been confusing us for months. Being in character means leaving our friendship behind and acting as if we're in love with each other. This stolen moment behind the tree, out of sight of the camp, is exactly something the two lovers would do, but it's also something Parker and Lisbeth would do.

Before he can answer, a trumpet blares, the signal for rehearsal. I thrust the rifle in his hands and give him a kiss on the cheek. My kiss apparently breaks him out of his thoughts, and he grins, clearly excited for what the next few days are going to bring. History's the one thing we both love and half a thousand people and counting isn't going to squash that.

"I'll take my leave then, Miss Lisbeth."

"Go on, Private, but return to me soon." I stifle a giggle watching him walk down the hill, rifle slung over his shoulder.

A deep rumble startles me awake. The next few are big enough that the pictures of my family and a few of Parker and me on my wall rattle. Heart pounding, I dress as quickly as I can in my costume: a plain brown dress, petticoats, an apron, and my trusty pair of boots. I pin up my hair, resisting the urge to braid it since I was told not to, and grab the bonnet that I won't wear anyway.

Mom's cooking eggs when I rush in for breakfast. School is cancelled for the two-day reenactment and other festivities. All three of my younger siblings sit at the table. Judging by their sleepy, sour faces, they resent me for the cannons that woke them up this early. The next oldest, Jesse, snickers when he sees me.

"Going for a walk on the prairie, Lisbeth?"

"Jesse!" Mom says. I grab a banana muffin out of the pantry and lean against the counter to eat it.

"At least Lisbeth goes outside and doesn't play video games instead of doing her homework."

Glancing at the clock on the microwave, I realize I'm going to be late and stuff the muffin in my apron pocket. The historical society is only a ten-minute walk, but I practically run. Nobody's at the door of the museum, which is the original city hall, but a line of people waiting for entry stretches down the block and disappears around the corner. I duck through the side entrance.

Dodging fresh daffodils and hoop skirts, I run into Mabel, vice president of the society. The president of the society, Ron, aka the colonel, is in the field and I'm to report to him later. Those two are the only people allowed to communicate with radios. The rest of us get to figure out what's going on, but that adds to the madness that today's going to be.

"You were nearly late, Miss Lisbeth."

I curtsy. "Apologies, ma'am. I woke up late. Where am I to be today?"

"Your job's to take notes for the newspaper, which means you'll be wandering around. Get as close to the battle as you dare, but not so close you'll be hurt. Understood?"

"Yes, ma'am."

"Good." She hands me a field journal, a pencil, and a small knife to sharpen it with. The notes will be for my project, but Mabel likes to get into character as early as possible. "Once the battle's over, you'll serve as a nurse."

"Yes, ma'am."

Turning away, Mabel orders one of the other girls to open the doors. Thunder rattles the china in the cupboards—the reenactment of Lil' Ol' Hill is underway.

My thoughts turn to Parker, as they often have over the past few months. Where is he? Is he going to get hurt by accident? How does he look in his uniform today? I shake that last thought out of my head, taking the muffin out of my pocket and eating it. The clamor of battle grows louder and more distinct as I climb the crescent-shaped hill from the opposite side. The rifles sound like fireworks and I can feel the cannon booms in my chest. I haven't even looked over the crest of the hill, where Confederate soldiers are trying to take back the town from the Union. Parker would be defending the hill, and the town, but I'm not allowed to get close. Not yet.

I climb the same oak tree he and I had been sitting under a couple days ago. From here, I have a good view of the gentle slope of the hill where most of the fighting is happening. Smoke from the field below drifts up toward me. My job in the project is to be part of the battle as a nurse later on, but for now, I'm discreetly taking notes, which could either be turned into an article or a diary entry. Others are either back at the museum, talking to tourists and taking pictures, or are participating in the battle as well.

Shouts draw my attention, battle cries and dying screams. I scribble as fast as I can, trying to choose my words as I would have if I lived in the 1800s, but it's difficult and I can always rewrite it later. The battle itself is distracting and I find myself climbing higher to get a better view. Shading my eyes with one hand, I hold onto the branch above me with the other. Something clicks, audibly clicks. At first I think it's the branch, but when I look down, it's one of my classmates in jeans and a light hoodie with a camera.

"What time is it?" I ask. I'm desperate to know something since the sun has hidden behind clouds. Last I checked, I thought it was about noon.

"One-thirty and here," she says, tossing up a sandwich and an apple. "Mabel said you left before getting a lunch."

I'm left alone again, writing notes and badly sketching the battle lines on the field. A trumpet blows somewhere, calling for a ceasefire, the signal to move on with the day. I head down to camp on the southern tip of the crescent, wondering whether Parker's still at the northern tip. Wondering whether he's thinking about me.

Nursing duty passes mostly without incident. I talk to tourists and soldiers alike, the former making it hard to keep a straight face since they continuously try to trip me up. Not once do I break character, even when I ask about Parker. "Have you seen Private Garcia today?"

"No, miss, I haven't seen him since the mornin'," comes the reply. "He might still be in the field, helping get the wounded here."

I pass the first aid tent as I'm coming back to camp from town with fresh bread from the bakery. Several soldiers sit around, their hands wrapped in gauze. One of them is holding an ice pack to his face.

"Would any of you fellas like a fresh piece of bread?" I ask. The one with the ice pack holds out his hand. "Why are y'all sitting around?"

"Accident with my gun," he says, ripping off a chunk with his teeth. He chews and swallows. "It's been a while since I've volunteered and I forgot about the recoil on the rifle. Got smacked right in the face."

"A cannon backfired and we were lucky that it only caught our hands," another soldier says. "It's not too bad."

"Y'all got hurt though," I say, still in character even though there's no civilians to be seen. The paramedic must've gone for more ice or water.

"Darlin', we do this kind of thing all the time," ice pack soldier laughs. I'm not entirely sure if he's still in character or not. "We know the dangers."

I continue on my way, searching for Parker. It's not like him to not show up to work and I start to worry that he got hurt. Yet whenever I walk past the first aid tent, he's not there. The one time I try to sneak away to the museum, someone comes running up with a message from the colonel saying I need to talk to the tourists. They wave me off when I ask about Parker, saying he likely got drafted into helping out at the museum since we're both original employees of the historical society and Mabel likely needed help.

Why she needs him instead of me, I can't answer. The colonel keeps me away from the camera crew who want to interview me, saying I'll have more time tomorrow. It's hard to imagine doing this all over again but then it'll be done with. Although, if it's a massive success, the town might want to stage another one; hopefully Parker and I will be off to our next adventure by then.

Parker still doesn't show up by dusk, and by then, it's time to go home and do it all again tomorrow. The day after, it's all about getting as many people in town as possible to watch the news crew's footage and to really enjoy all our town has to offer. If I can get through that without snapping at a mom with her three whiny kids, it'll be a miracle.

Later that night, I'm in my room typing up my notes from the day when there's a knock on the front door and I hear Mom say, "Parker! What happened to you?"

"It's nothing, Ma. Is Lisbeth upstairs?"

"She is, go on up."

The old wooden stairs creak. "Parker, can you help me with my Spanish project? I have to talk about Costa Rica and I remembered your family is from there."

"Later, Jesse. I'm here to see your sister."

He opens my door and waits for me to notice. When I look up at him, he has a bandage peeking through the black of his hair on his forehead and one on his chin. "What the hell?"

One of my little sisters happens to walk by at that moment. "Mommy, Lisbeth said a bad word!"

"Just take the quarter for the jar instead of tattling." I shove a coin in her hand and close the door. "Seriously, Parker, what the hell?"

"It's nothing, Lis. Here, I'll show you." Parker peels off the tape and lifts the gauze on his forehead. The gash isn't deep, but it still looks angry and red. His chin looks a lot like the scrape he got last summer when he fell off his skateboard. "See, I'm fine."

"How did you get hurt? I didn't see you at the first aid tent." We sit on the floor, backs resting against my bed, our legs intertwined in front of us. It feels right, though our relationship has shifted without us really becoming aware of it until a few weeks ago when rehearsals became more frequent. Whenever we showed affection to each other, be it a hand on my back or a kiss on the cheek, I felt a rush that wasn't there before. One time, I caught Parker watching me when he thought I wasn't looking, and he had the look that Disney princes give their princesses before kissing them.

"It was an accident. The chin is a burn from my rifle, because I was careless and rested it against my face after I fired it. A volunteer hit me with his bayonet when we were called to attention in ranks. They patched me up just before the ceasefire sounded. I was told to help out in the museum instead of going to camp."

"Aren't the bayonets blunted?"

"Yeah, but he tossed it up with enough force to give me a gash." He shifts to put an arm around me and I burrow into his side. His fingers absently drum on my arm and the touch sends tingles down my spine.

"You have to be careful." I lay my head on his shoulder, listening to his heart. It beats faster when I put a hand on his chest. A warmth settles in my stomach when he starts to play with my hair. "Several people were at the first aid tent for gunpowder burns. Even with all of the practice, things can still go wrong."

"You don't have to worry, I'll be fine."

"You're leading the charge tomorrow." Twisting, I end up straddling his lap with his hands on my hips. We've been pushing the boundaries between us, but this is the closest we've gotten to anything resembling being romantic with each other. My hair forms a wall of chestnut brown around us as I lean closer and whisper, "Of course I'm going to worry about you."

"Like I said, I'll be fine," he whispers, hands traveling up and down my back. The Disney look appears again on Parker's face and he eventually pulls me in for a gentle kiss.

Not a second after we pull apart, there's a knock at the door and Jesse says, "Can Parker help me with my project now?"

"Later, Jesse!" We say at the same time. He stomps away and I start laughing, which gets Parker going. It's a while before we settle down; the laughter trails off into the cheesy, looking-into-each-other's-eyes crap. And as aware of that as I am, it makes it no less thrilling to hear him say, "Hey."

"Hey." I go to kiss him again but there's another knock at the door.

"Lisbeth, Parker, it's getting late and you've got another busy day tomorrow! Parker should leave now so you can get enough sleep."

We scramble to our feet and Parker throws on his jacket while I go to open the door. He stops me by grabbing my arm and spinning me around for a quick kiss. "I'll talk to you tomorrow, ok?"

He's gone before I can even suggest calling him instead.

Same tree. Notebook. Pencil. The lunch Mabel pushed into my hands. Scribbling, watching, listening. Waiting for the tide to turn, for the Confederate soldiers to almost make it up the hill before the Union side sends them back down. Like yesterday, I try to find Parker, but it's hopeless. But unlike yesterday, I have the memory of the kiss from last night, and I daydream about stealing a moment later. Or kissing him as soon as I see him. I really am turning into that sweetheart, and I'm not sure how to get past it.

I can hardly hear the drums over the gunshots and cannons, but then the trumpets sound a charge. This is it, the moment where things could go horribly wrong and Parker's in the middle of it. From my vantage point, I see grey sweep up the slope, almost overrunning the blues hiding behind trees and in small trenches. But then, a brave blue vaults over the line, shoving his way through with his rifle. The rest follow suit, and it looks as though they're actually fighting and bleeding and dying. That first blue, Private Garcia, my Parker, gets swallowed up and I can't distinguish him from everyone else.

More trumpets call for a retreat: my cue to get to camp. Shoving things into my pockets, I jump down, and it feels as though the yelling is louder, the screams more piercing. The cannon catches me off guard and I press a hand to my chest like an actual southern belle. There's a need to do my job, but also a need to find Parker. In my haze, I step on a forgotten baseball and twist my ankle. Momentum carries me down the hill and I lay there, dazed, and take stock of my surroundings.

Smoke still floats atop the grass. Moaning, I pick myself up and put weight on my foot. Pain races up my leg and I crumple back to the ground. Through the haze, shapes materialize. Colors bleed through, blue and gray mixing together, and bodies solidify. The field is quiet save for the drums in the distance beating a ceasefire, and I realize it's the first time in hours that my heart isn't pounding from the cannons. It starts up again as those pretending to be dead are reborn and the bodies move. I need to find Parker.

When I scream his name, the sound carries through the silence. He could be hurt, though great precautions have been taken to minimize that risk. All rifles and cannons fired blanks, though some volunteers, as well as Parker, did get hurt yesterday. And I did just roll down the hill because some kid lost a baseball.

"Miss Lisbeth, what are you doin' here? Ain't you supposed to be at camp?" A soldier kneels down next to me. I can't tell the color of his uniform because it's soaked in blood or whatever equivalent we used.

"Where's Parker?" At this point, I'm crying from the fear and the pain.

"He oughta be at camp by now since he's the one who led the charge. Are you hurt?"

I nod, gesturing to my ankle. He barks an order to another soldier and they help me up. We head back to camp, weaving through men who shake their heads, trying to clear the ringing from their ears. Many are still on the ground, dead or injured, while the stretchers rush in. The news crew with their cameras are stationed right at the edge of the field and we ignore their shouts for an interview.

They bring me to the first aid tent, where more soldiers sit than the day before. Some have gunpowder burns and others overextended themselves while running, the type of injuries that those in the field would be faking. I put some weight on my foot. It doesn't hurt as much, and after I'm examined, the paramedic says I didn't sprain my ankle but I should take it easy and stick around camp. I'm given some painkillers and I swallow them with water as the paramedic wraps my ankle.

I limp to the nurses' tent, taking note of how busy the camp is. Several nurses and surgeons buzz about, getting ready for the onslaught of soldiers, and I can hear the colonel's voice booming from somewhere. Two women sit inside the tent, taking a break from the action, and don't notice me coming inside. I find an empty seat and sink into it even though it's made of wood. They look over.

"What happened to you?" one asks.

"I fell down the hill because a stupid kid left their baseball in the grass." I pull the pins out of my hair and quickly braid two plaits, pinning them to the back of my head. "When are they bringing in the injured?"

"Anytime now. Can you work?"

I stand and lean on the foot. It's stiff now, thanks to the wrap and my boot. "I can manage."

Another nurse pops her head into the tent. "Lisbeth, there you are! The colonel wants you to do a quick check of the tents to make sure they're good to go."

"Of course."

All I have to do is lift the flap and make sure everything looks right. A few of the tents will be left empty for the public to fully explore, but the others will be filled with soldiers and surgeons and nurses. As soon as I leave one tent, people scurry in, unload a body, and scurry back out again. The soldiers call for water and comfort, but I can't give either to them, even after I'm finished checking the tents. I don't want to come across Parker, despite his reassurances that nothing would happen to him. He was already hurt once, and with the first aid tent filling up, I'm scared it's going to happen again.

My next set of orders are to direct stretchers to empty beds or to the "operating theater," an open-air tent where volunteers patch up fake wounds. An hour or so passes and I haven't seen a trace of Parker. Thoughts of him writhing in actual pain crowd my mind, and suddenly every person I see is him until I'm running through camp, ignoring the pain flaring in my foot with each step.

People call out, but I don't stop, dodging several tourists and the weary soldiers who walked in on their own. The colonel's tent is right there; he'll know where Parker is. A tour group arrives, standing right in front of the flaps, and I almost force my way through them when I hear "Lisbeth!"

And there he is, mud splattering his legs, hair stuck to his forehead, covered in dirt, but he's there. I reach out for him and we grab each other's arms before Parker swings me up into the air, laughing, and I laugh too, tears falling down my face. I hear cheers and applause in the background, but it doesn't matter. He sets me down and hugs me tightly, whispering, "I've never felt so terrified in my life. It felt so real."

"I felt it too," I say, not wanting to let go. "Especially after I fell down the hill."

"What? How?" He pulls back, inspecting me. The gash on his forehead has split open and there's a new crust of dry blood mixed with dirt, but he's uninjured as far as I can tell. I reach up and straighten his cap, knocking off some dirt in the process.

"Private Garcia and Miss Phillips!" The tent flaps open and the colonel steps out. Parker and I split apart. "Need I remind you about your duties? Go!"

We both struggle to hold back smiles and salute. The colonel turns to the tour group, and Parker winks at me. We're conscious once again of the roles we have to play, but that doesn't stop me from giving him a kiss on his cheek, since that's what a sweetheart would do.

Over the next week or so, I somehow piece together a short summary of my experience during the reenactment. The classmate who took my photo gives me a copy. She captured me on my tiptoes, leaning over the ground, grasping the branch overhead for balance, the other hand shading my eyes. My dress ripples a bit in the breeze, and the bonnet dangles from a twig, forgotten.

I include that one in my report but there's a series of photos I keep for myself. Soon, they'll accompany me across the states to a university in Massachusetts, along with Parker. Another photographer captured the moment we found each other after the battle, charging toward each other from opposite ends of the frame. My eyes gleam with tears though I have the biggest smile on my face. Relief is etched into the mud and blood from the scabs on Parker's face. Our arms reach for each other, our fingers just shy of connecting. The fear isn't completely gone from my face, not until the next shot with my eyes squeezed shut as Parker sets me back down.

The final photo is a close-up of me: face freckled and tear-streaked, hair again in disarray, but smiling as I brush some dirt off of Parker's cap.

LAKE SUPERIOR RADIO: ON BOXING DAY

S. Alastor Node

Cheese makes the dog fart.

Our golden prefers sneaking up on us—or, more precisely, our food—all catlike when we aren't looking, snout leading the rest of its white-cream-beige body to whatever has been left carelessly on the table. The dog isn't young enough to put its fur-tasseled paws up, but the coffee table is fair game.

Snake has always done her work on the coffee table, ever since that first piece of homework when she was in grade school and still Suzy Sullivan. She sits Indian-style on the gray wooden floor as she types, bitten-down fingernails illuminated by the backlit keyboard. There is, admittedly, something to be said about cold floors in the hot Michigan summers and colder floors in the winter, although that doesn't seem as fun, but summer habits are hard to break. After all, I still squat outside every three hours, cigarette in shivering hand, the edge of my thinning coat brushing the snow my boots had pushed through.

Snake's body is swathed in blankets, the latest torn free from under the Christmas tree, but her feet are bare, toenails bright against the pale wooden floor. They're red and neon green on alternating toes, as if she's twelve all over again. The dog's wet nose finds its way onto the coffee table, but it's 2019 and there's no paper to eat anymore. Snake reaches over and absentmindedly scratches the bridge of that wet brown nose between wet brown eyes. They blink once, twice, three times. Then the dog lumbers laboriously around the coffee table, between the couches, and settles onto Snake's Christmas blanket.

The dog isn't much of a fan of Christmas. There are plenty of smells to go around, plenty of missed moments when no one is watching the cookies on the table or the muffins that are too close to the edge of the end table, but goddamn the wrapping paper. Goddamn the wrapping paper. That was what banished it down to the basement after all. When Snake was younger, and so was the dog, there was a whole day where we waited for the goddamn wrapping paper to appear in the dog's poop. It hadn't been a very fun Christmas for any of us, and it resulted in a dog ban on Christmas day. Auntie always said, till the day she died, that she couldn't get the smell of dog poop out of her nose on Christmas. I myself always find it somewhere between the smell of peppermint coffee and cinnamon rolls, a ghost of a scent brought on by memory. The dog hadn't pooped out the wrapping paper. It had, however, burped not long after Snake had sworn that she'd seen a little bit of glitter come out of that gaping pink maw.

My sister, for many years, seemed to share the same view of Christmas as the dog did. Presents were fun enough but there'd always be a couple hours when Snake would vanish. Worn out from the family bonding, she'd disappear into the depths of her room or, once she was old enough to be alone after dark, out the back door. Auntie had tutted the first time, but no one said anything after that. They just sipped on Jack, called it eggnog, and watched National Lampoon's Christmas Vacation. The kids got milk with a spot of coffee and a heaping mound of whipped cream. Everyone brushed white dog hairs off their tongues.

Snake would wander around town, hatless, and walk onto the pier that she wasn't supposed to walk onto in the winter. Then, and only then, would she return to us with snowflakes dotting her gloomy hair. She'd give a cheery hello, her head blocking the wall clock with its small hand on the curved number nine, and hand the dog a stick from some new exotic location so it could chew on that instead of whatever else had the misfortune to be left on the floor. Nine o'clock—that was Snake's family time renewed. Her eyes would dance, and she'd laugh with Auntie and Gammie and Cousin Cailyn (who wasn't our cousin, but Gammie's). She'd go to bed at ten that night.

It'd never been strange when Snake was a child that there were no men, and it was so normal by the time she'd become an adult that it was taxing to consider the thought. Although, to be fair, by the time she was an adult most of the *real* adults that'd raised us had died off. Cousin Cailyn had been the last to go, buried in the ground next to Gammie and Auntie and all the others Snake had never been acquainted with. Christmases became a little easier after that, if only because now no one would raise eyebrows at how much Jack we put into our mugs. Of course, the family was missed—that couldn't be helped—but we had each other for the most part. Snake still went on her expeditions, but that didn't seem like it would change even if the living status of our only family did. It hadn't mattered much after that whether there were men in the family or not, because really, there was no one except us and the dog.

Every year, the dog remembered the scents of the faraway places Snake went to, places it probably couldn't quite imagine but smelled nevertheless. Dog imaginations aren't very good. There weren't just the smells from the gifts Snake brought back home for it, of course, because whiffs of the Outside were woven into my sister's winter coat and her slightly moist socks and her scarf, which she'd remember even though she always forget her hat. Even in 2019, Snake remains the same—she hates those hats—and even in 2019 the dog finds those smells bark-worthy. The dog has always barked, no matter what the occasion, but for Christmas this year it was from the air from just outside town that lingered in the creases of Snake's coat. Although, to be fair, it could just as likely have been the smell of irony train tracks covered in snow woven into the cuffs of her socks. Or perhaps the scent of some stranger's car Snake sat in on her way back that had settled into each purl of the multicolored scarf around her neck. Certainly, it could've been anything; the dog just liked to bark. It tried to sound them out as well as it could with its little domed head so it could understand. The stick Snake handed the dog this year had the smell of the homeless man all over it, and the dog had always loved that fresh homeless man smell, since the very beginning, in the summer of '08.

When it's sunny we remember the dog as a puppy—a small tyrant of a thing that loved to get into trouble as much as it loved the things the cat swiped off the table and onto the ground. The cat's name was Robert, a name that had started as a joke, even though Robert had no balls to warrant such a masculine name, and no bipedalism to warrant such a human one. Maybe that's why she was so mean all the time—out of pure spite for such a terrible name. Lord knows Snake fought her own nickname for years before finally giving in (we gave it to her because of her peculiar amber eyes and sharp tongue.)

That cat was old, old, old. It was our first female to go down, and the nastiest of the lot. Snake loved cats but even she couldn't stand Robert. Robert loved to get the dog, back when it was a puppy, in trouble. There was something about sad retriever eyes that seemed to fill Robert with joy, the mean old thing. The dog always got it back, though, with a little nip of the tail, or—and this was its favorite thing to do—by barreling into the cat when dinnertime came along. It's an astonishing thing that Robert lived as long as she did.

The dog had been the reason Snake started going barefoot. Little white hairs on the ground made it too hard to wear socks. Also, it didn't make sense to make fun of the dog for sliding on the wooden floor with its furry paws if we slid around in our socks too. There was a point in pressing the human advantage.

Snake and the dog used to bunk together when the dog first got here in the summer, when she was twelve, until they both got too big to sleep in the same bed. Well, "bed" is stretching it. In any case, the dog didn't like its dog bed and my sister didn't like her futon. So, a year after we'd gotten the dog, Snake started wearing training bras and acquired a queen-size, while the dog sulked around the house on account of the thrown-away futon and never slept in the same bed as Snake ever again. Be that as it may, Snake persisted in sleeping curled up in the corner of the queen-size. Summer habits are hard to break.

Snake stretches, fingers reaching for something unknown, thrown back from her shoulders as if she's about to take flight. The fuzzy blanket drops off her shoulder and falls over the dog. It's snowing outside and she turns to look at the snow while the golden traps itself further in the blanket. We hadn't had a white Christmas in ages, and she tells me so.

"It's not Christmas, Suzette. It's Boxing Day."

She makes a face and goes back to typing busily on her laptop. The dog growls and mummifies itself further in its unfortunate wrappings. It pulls the blanket out from under Snake and her toes slam onto the bare floor. She yelps as the cold seeps into her skin. She smacks my arm when I laugh, startling me so much that I drop my grilled cheese on the ground. As it turns out, food is a great instigator for the disentanglement of a golden retriever.

The air is sulfurous till what seems like May.

ACKNOWLEDGMENTS

To my family and friends for your support, love, and encouragement, the laughs, the revisions, and for lighting the spark of belief in my writing. And this book wouldn't be complete without a huge thank you to all the Writers' Community members who put your work in our manuscript when it was just a wishful thought. Thank you.

— Kathryn Orwig

Thank you Kristin, Michael, Tish, and Jeremy for believing in me.

— J.D. Akins

To my family and friends for the encouragement and support even though I never let you read my work and to my professors and classmates for the constructive criticism during workshop when I had to share my work. These stories were a group effort.

— Ivy Obuchowski

To family for making me a reader, to friends for making me a writer, and to those many afternoons we had at the defunct Espresso Royale on State St. for making me feel like I belong.

— Carol May

To my friends and family who have encouraged me every step of the way.

— Kaleb A. Brown

To my parents, and to my most cherished friends Chloe and Christina, who inspire me—through all of life's hardships—to keep writing.

— L.L. Renno

To Cecil, for showing me the strength in persistence, to my friends for their constant encouragement even though I never tell you what I'm doing, and to my siblings for always thinking I'm cool despite the many times I prove you wrong.

— Abby O'Meara

To family and friends, to Sandy and Ayisha who encouraged me to love creative writing, and to Mickey, whose love and support have always uplifted me.

— C.D. GIllikin

To my family, for always being there, and to everyone else who encouraged and supported me along the way.

— Lila Scott

To my Amma, for being the perfect muse, to my cat, for simply being, and to my new dog friend, Muffet. Stories of your adventures and your big, golden retriever heart will always be told. Oh, and to dairy, for making the dog fart. I couldn't have written that story without you.

— S. Alastor Node

THE WRITERS' COMMUNITY

Authors

KATHRYN ORWIG can be found in coffee shops writing about Marble Rollers, Dream Chasers, and Queens who were never born to wear a crown. From film and TV scripts to novels, poetry, and short stories, she enjoys writing everything and anything. Kathryn graduated from the University of Michigan with a B.A. in Creative Writing and minors in Russian and Russian Studies. She won a Hopwood Award in 2017, won the Seattle National Film Festival for Talented Youth's Best Screenplay Competition in 2018, earned a Top 25 and Top 10 placement in the Barnstorm and Women in Horror Film Festival Competitions in 2019 and 2020, respectively. More of her work can be found at kathrynorwig.com

J.D. AKINS is rumored to be an amateur author operating in the Ann Arbor area. Reports allege that he is currently working on an undergraduate B.A. in English. One eyewitness statement claims that he enjoys writing short stories, radio dramas, and attempts at novels about spaceship captains, superheroes, or maybe the occasional wizard. This anthology supposedly contains his first-ever published works, which he hopes to be the first of many.

IVY OBUCHOWSKI divides her time between writing, reading, and spending time outdoors despite sunburning easily and always bitten by insects. She graduated with a B.S. in the Environment focusing on conservation and wildlife with a minor in Creative Writing from the University of Michigan. This is her first publishing endeavor and looks forward to more in the future.

CAROL MAY inhabits the same material realm that the rest of you do (as far as she's aware anyway). Her stories have never been published before. Congratulations, you are one of the lucky ones that gets to start this whole writing journey with her. She doesn't know what she's doing and she's got a degree to prove it! With a recently acquired University of Michigan B.S. in Earth Science along with a minor in Linguistics, she thinks a little too much about the future and a lot too much on what to write next. [Insert mention of giving hugs to her cute cat named Oreo here to instill endearment toward her to anyone who happens to be reading here].

It's a bird, it's a plane! It's the next best thing hoping to be the next big thing: **KALEB A. BROWN**. Kaleb aims to one day make a splash by writing novels that ditch the humdrum of our lives whilst dealing with the big emotions that we find ourselves grappling with. That isn't to say Kaleb's a one-trick pony: Kaleb writes short stories, poems, reviews, and journalism pieces. Most recently, he's had his work published at the Detroit Free Press. He works toward a B.A. in Creative Writing, minoring in Global Media Studies and History. When he's not writing or doing assignments (which is to say, hardly ever), he mostly likes to spend his time watching anime, reading novels, and playing video games.

L.L. RENNO, real name Lucas Renno, is an author and screenwriter with a particular focus on speculative and fantasy fiction. In his stories, he strives to create worlds that feel vast, alive, and—above all—real, while at the same time taking care to not lose focus of the numerous colorful characters that inhabit them. Despite this predilection toward worldbuilding, Renno is also perfectly at home creating stories set in our world and our times, often drawing heavily on his own numerous experiences in order to create the optimal story to make one simultaneously laugh and cry. When not writing, Renno can often be found in the kitchen honing his skill as a chef and baker, or in front of his computer at 3 in the morning reading random articles on Wikipedia.

ABBY O'MEARA is a theoretical being who is reportedly studying toward a B.S. in microbiology and a minor in Chinese Language and Culture, and also manages to sometimes write in their spare time. They enjoy writing novels and short stories, although they mysteriously all end up in various unfinished states. They supposedly had a poem published in middle school, though this is their first proper publishing experience.

C.D. GILLIKIN is the name given to a large bipedal primate that can sometimes be found in the forests and swamps of the Great Lakes area. Long suspected to be able to use tools like the other apes, some zoopsychologists have held to the once-fringe idea that it is capable of creating speculative fiction and deriving a sense of wonder and beauty from its odd roaming about in nature. While piano music has been heard drifting from its alleged den, the text within this tome provides the first published evidence of its ability to create.

LILA SCOTT is a senior at the University of Michigan, studying German and Economics. She loves coffee, reading, and white wine, among all the other fine things in life. She could probably beat you at Jeopardy, but would definitely lose at Monopoly. Her favorite species of animal is dog, and as evidenced by this anthology, she has written at least one poem.

S. ALASTOR NODE was unfortunately born in Ohio but uses this misfortune to write about Michigan and her mother instead. A senior at the University of Michigan, she is majoring in Philosophy and English and hopes to be a professor one day. Often, she wonders if her students will find this book and, if they do, how they'd react to knowing that 42° 15' 19.224" N 83° 41' 13.92" W once sparked joy.

CPSIA information can be obtained
at www.ICGtesting.com
Printed in the USA
LVHW100238270422
717347LV00003B/53

9 781947 989740